12 DAYS OF WINTER

By Stuart MacBride

The Logan McRae Novels
Cold Granite
Dying Light
Broken Skin
Flesh House
Blind Eye
Dark Blood
Shatter the Bones
Close to the Bone

Other Works
Sawbones
Birthdays for the Dead

Writing as Stuart B. MacBride
Halfhead

STUART MACBRIDE

12 DAYS OF WINTER

HarperCollins*Publishers*

HarperCollins*Publishers*
77–85 Fulham Palace Road,
Hammersmith, London W6 8JB

www.harpercollins.co.uk

Published by HarperCollins*Publishers* 2012
1

A catalogue record for this book
is available from the British Library

ISBN: 978-0-00-750290-5

Set in Meridien by Palimpsest Book Production Limited,
Falkirk, Stirlingshire
Printed and bound in Great Britain by
Clays Ltd, St Ives plc

For Al, Donna, and Ed

1: A Partridge in a Pear Tree

Billy Partridge wasn't really cut out to be a cat burglar, but Dillon hadn't really given him any option. It was either do the job, or come up with thirteen grand by Thursday . . . or have both legs shattered. And the leg thing didn't even write-off what they owed Dillon, just deferred the interest. Come the 15th of January, there'd still be thirteen thousand to pay.

Grunting, Billy hoisted himself further up the tree, his XXL designer jeans smeared with moss and dirt. That's what he got for trusting Twitch to bring the sodding stepladder.

Of course, *Twitch* didn't need a stepladder. He'd clambered over the outside wall like a bloody monkey, so the old oak tree growing close to the manor house hadn't been much of a challenge. Even if it was strung all over with heavy-duty Christmas lights. But then Twitch looked like a collection of manky coat hangers – dressed up in drainpipe trousers, baseball cap and camouflage hoodie – not a single ounce of spare flesh on him, while Billy had to haul twenty-one stone of asthmatic underachiever from branch to branch, wheezing like his lungs were about to explode.

He struggled up to the same branch as Twitch, right outside a darkened window. Billy hugged the trunk, stuck his head against the bark, puffing and panting. 'Ah. . . Ah, Jesus . . . Jesus Christ. . .'

'Thought you was gonnae peg out on me, like.' Twitch tried for a wink. Not easy with a pair of panda-black eyes and a freshly broken nose: Dillon 'reminding' them not to screw this one up.

'You could have bloody helped!'

Twitch grinned, his teeth manky brown in the shadow of his baseball cap and hooded top. 'Looked like you needed the fuckin' exercise.'

Billy *didn't* need the exercise. Billy needed a joint and a packet of Jaffa Cakes. But not till they'd got in, got the painting, and got the hell out before anyone called the police, or 'released the hounds'. It was that kind of place.

From up here, in the tree, Billy had a perfect view all the way down Fletcher Road: big Victorian sandstone piles with huge gardens, festooned with discreetly shimmering white lights. None of your inflatable Santas and flashing snowmen here – nah, this was where Oldcastle's old money lived. With a fine view of the Bellows and the Kings River, Castle Hill was *not* for the likes of Fat Billy Partridge and Andy 'Twitch' McKay.

'Well?' said Billy. 'We going to do this or not?'

'Aye, aye, hud yer horses.' Twitch pulled out a knife, leaned across the gap between the branch and the building,

2

and wheegled the blade in between the top part of the sash window and the bottom, keeping the sound of splintering wood to a minimum. How come rich bastards couldn't stretch to double glazing? Billy and his mum might be living in a crappy council semi by the North Station tracks, but at least they had double-bloody-glazing.

Twitch eased the blade back and forth until something inside went *click*. 'Bingo.' He grinned again. 'OK, you ready?'

'I was born ready.'

'You were born a fat bastard.'

Billy scowled at him. 'Shut up.'

'You shut up.'

'Oh for God's sake. . .' Billy grabbed the bottom part of the window and hauled it up, gritting his teeth as the ancient wood squealed.

Twitch gave him a slow round of applause. 'Oh, my hero: you're so big and *strong*!'

Billy kept his voice low, going for a Clint Eastwood growl and failing miserably. 'You want us to get caught? That what you want? You want to go back to prison? No?' He gave the sarky bastard a wee shove. 'Then shut up and get your arse in there.'

Twitch pursed his lips. 'Don't be such a gaywad. Dillon said they were both deaf as a post. . .' He slipped inside like a shadow.

Billy took a deep breath, said a wee prayer, then scrambled across the yawning chasm into the house. Didn't look down. Didn't fall to his death. Didn't crap himself.

From the outside, Number Seven Fletcher Road looked all prosperous and well maintained, but the foosty smelling room Billy clambered into was piled with old boxes and tea chests, all just visible in the dim glow of the garden's Christmas lights, and—

MONSTER!

Billy grabbed the window ledge, heart trying to kick its way out of his chest. They were going to die. . .

No. Not a monster: a full-sized stuffed black bear leaned back against the wall at an alarming angle, next to a grandfather clock and a suit of armour. Creepy bastard taxidermy lurking in the shadows.

'Look at this!' Twitch dug into a box and pulled out a pair of matching African masks, like they had on the Discovery Channel. 'These have to be worth a bob or two.'

Billy snatched them off him and stuffed them back where they'd come from. 'Don't be an arse: everything in here's junk. If it wasn't they wouldn't keep it in this shite hole.'

He opened the door a crack and peered out into the corridor. Dark and empty, faded rectangles on the wallpaper marking where paintings used to be. No carpet, no furniture. Light spilled up the stairwell from the floors below, the tip of a huge Christmas tree almost coming level with the balustrade. The tree was festooned with shimmering white lights – like the garden – and covered in burgundy and gold baubles, ribbons and swags. A wee bit swankier than the four-foot high artificial thing clarted with pink and blue tinsel in Billy's living room.

A television blared out *Britain's Next Big Star* from somewhere below as Billy and Twitch crept from room to room.

The whole place was vacant bordering on the derelict . . . except for the room nearest the stairs. It had been done out as a study, the walls lined with books, and a desk facing the window complete with fancy-looking laptop and colour printer.

Twitch rubbed his skeletal hands together. 'Payday.' He grabbed the laptop, pulling up all the cables and wrapping them round the thing before squeezing it into a leather case he found beside the desk. 'That's *got* to be worth a couple of hundred down the Monk and Casket!' He went for a high five, but Billy missed. Twitch shook his head, slung the case over his shoulder. 'Last one downstairs is a fat poofy bastard.'

They snuck down to the middle floor. This bit of the house had more of a lived-in feel: carpets, sideboards, occasional tables, framed photographs. Six doors led off the corridor and they picked their way through them carefully, making as little noise as possible, even though there was bugger-all chance anyone could hear anything over the TV. Four dusty guest bedrooms with fading wallpaper, a huge, cold bathroom.

Billy eased the final door open and peered inside: must be the master bedroom. Breathy snoring came from a large divan bed. A white-haired woman lay flat on her back in the darkness, wearing one of them sleeping masks, surrounded by a nest of frilly pillows.

He scanned the walls. No sign of the painting.

Time to close up, move on, and— 'Hoy!'

Twitch squeezed past him, into the room. Billy grabbed at his sleeve but the wee sod was too quick.

Billy shifted from foot to foot on the threshold, voice a sharp-edged whisper. 'What the hell do you think you're doing? Come back here!'

But Twitch wasn't listening, he was rummaging through

the old lady's drawers, pulling out camisole knickers and support stockings, letting them fall to the swirly carpet. 'Shut up and watch the corridor.'

'We're going to get caught!'

'You are such a fat. . .' Twitch paused, smiled, then pulled a wooden box out of the bottom drawer. He cracked it open and the smile got even bigger. 'Ya beauty!' He scurried back to the door and showed Billy what was inside.

'Fuck me.' Gold and silver and diamonds: necklaces, rings, earrings, and a couple of watches.

'See: you stick with your uncle Twitch, he'll see you right.' He shut the door, licking his lips as he fingered the rings out in the corridor. 'This'll keep Dillon off our backs for a bit. How about you and me bugger off out of it while we're ahead?'

Billy fidgeted, looking from the glittering jewellery to Twitch's two black eyes and squint nose. Dillon's instructions had been *very* clear. 'He said we have to get the painting: if we don't he's going to break our legs.'

'But—'

'You *want* him to give you another spanking?'

Twitch sighed, then closed the wooden box. 'Maybe not.'

Billy squared his wide shoulders. 'Let's do it. . .'

They inched down to the ground floor.

The massive Christmas tree dominated the front lobby. Gifts were piled round the base: all multicoloured and shiny with bows and ribbons, like something out of Harry Fucking Potter. Be lucky if Billy's mum stretched to a selection box and a pair of socks this year, and these sods had all this? How was that fair? Rich bastard deserved to get his painting stolen. Serve him right.

6

Billy made Twitch hide behind the tree and keep an eye on the lounge, while he checked out the rooms on the ground floor: kitchen, cloakroom, drawing room, sun lounge, conservatory. . .

The painting was in the dining room. A large teak table sat in the middle, surrounded by a dozen fancy-looking chairs and a sideboard covered with silverware. A glass cabinet opposite the door was full of *objets d'art*: porcelain terriers, glass swans, ceramic clowns – that kinda thing. Some of which Billy's mum was going to find under their crappy plastic tree on Christmas day. Grinning, he helped himself, slipping the choicer looking pieces in his hoodie's pockets. And then it was painting time.

Dillon had given them a big holdall to put it in and Billy unrolled the thing and spread it out on the dining table. Then he turned the torch on the painting. And everything stopped.

A pear tree stood in the middle of a canvas as big as a widescreen telly – the leaves a mixture of delicate greens and dark blue, tinged with purple; the sky a riot of vermillion, ultramarine and gold as the sun set. And in the branches a single pear glistened. It was the most beautiful thing he'd ever seen in his life.

He was still standing there, mouth hanging open like a total mong, when Twitch shuffled into the room. 'What the flying fuck on a bike's taking you so long, Fatwad? And are those candlesticks gold, 'cause I'm having them if they are!'

Slowly Billy came back to earth. The mood was ruined, but the painting still called to him like it was wired right into his bloodstream: like the first joint of the day, or an armful of smack. . . No wonder Dillon was willing to write off their debt. According to the little brass plaque on the ornate gilded frame, this was THE PEAR TREE BY CLAUDE OSCAR MONET – 1907. Thirteen grand? This had to be worth *millions*.

Billy reached out and lifted the painting off its hook, not even daring to breathe as he lowered it into the unfurled holdall. It almost hurt to zip it up.

There was a clink from the sideboard. 'Now that's more like it!' Twitch stood up, clutching four bottles: Bombay Sapphire, Smirnoff, Talisker, and Courvoisier, wiggling his hips. 'We're on the bevy tonight.' He gyrated to a halt. 'What? You look like someone's crapped in your porridge.'

'Nothin'.' Billy picked up the holdall, clenched his jaw, ground his teeth. 'Let's get out of here.' It wasn't fair – why should Dillon get the painting? What the hell did *he* know about art? Nothing, that's what. Sweet bugger all. Dillon wouldn't have a clue how to appreciate something that beautiful. Dillon was a wanker with a line in drugs and violence. *Billy* had a GCSE in art – got a 'B' too – by rights the painting should be his.

He followed Twitch out into the hallway. Yeah: should be his. . .

Suppose he just kept it? Suppose Dillon didn't get the real painting, suppose Dillon got a fake instead? Billy's sister Susan fancied herself as a bit of an artist, she was always doing those 'paint by numbers' things.

Nah, it was a shite plan. That picture she did of some penguins looked more like vultures in dinner jackets. She'd just screw it up. Susan was stupid.

The television was still blaring away as they passed the huge Christmas tree – Twitch helped himself to a couple

8

of the presents underneath it, slipping them into his backpack.

Maybe. . . Maybe Dillon could have an accident? A smile split across Billy's face. Yeah, Dillon has an 'accident', their thirteen grand debt suddenly disappears, and Billy gets to keep Monet's *The Pear Tree*. Put it up on his bedroom wall, smoke some weed and look at the colours. *Sweet*.

He followed Twitch up the stairs. What kind of accident should Dillon have: car crash? Down the stairs? Back of the head caved in with a claw hammer? Claw hammer was probably best, that way Billy could just nip around to Dillon's flat, *pretend* to hand over the picture . . . and BANG! Soon as his back's turned. Maybe there'd even be some stuff lying about? Big bag of weed and a wad of—

A plummy, public-school voice bellowed out from the foot of the stairs. 'What the hell do you think you're doing?'

Twitch Froze. 'Fuck!' Then they legged it, hammering up the stairs two at a time.

The old bastard ran after them. He was one of those smoking jacket and silvery hair types, but he could move. 'Come back here!'

Billy nearly lost it on the last flight of stairs, but somehow managed to scrabble upright, bashing into the faded wallpaper, puffing and wheezing. Twitch screeched round the corner into the room with the stuffed black bear and the African masks.

A hand wrapped itself round Billy's arm and he squealed, span round and flailed out a fist. Pain sparked across his knuckles and the old guy grunted. Falling back. Giving Billy just enough time to scarper through the door

9

to the room they'd broken into, with all its boxes of junk. Billy shoved the stuffed bear, sending it clattering against the door. He leapt a cardboard box full of creepy china dolls and jumped for the window.

Bang!

He was lying on his back, staring up at the ceiling, wondering why everything hurt.

Bloody idiot: the painting's frame was too big to go through the gap straight on.

The door rattled. Billy struggled with the large, painting-filled holdall, working it round onto the diagonal, easing it through the open window. 'Andy!'

Twitch froze, halfway down the oak tree outside, glowering up at him, black eyes glittering in the Christmas lights. 'Don't use my real name!'

'Catch!' Billy swung the painting out and let go. It got halfway. There was a loud ripping sound as the holdall caught on a branch. A huge triangle of fabric tore free. The holdall dropped four feet, snagged on something, and hung there, swinging. The pear tree glowed through the jagged-edged hole, thirty foot over the frosty ground.

A loud thump from the hallway and the black bear lurched. BANG: it lurched again. One more time and the door crashed open. The old guy charged across the room. 'Bring back my bloody laptop!'

Billy crawled out onto the ledge and jumped for the nearest branch, just as a hand grabbed his ankle. Caught half over the gap, Billy twisted, didn't quite make it, banged his chin on the branch. He bit a big chunk out of his bottom lip; blood filled his mouth.

He scrabbled for purchase on the rough wood, but it was too late: he was falling, tangled up in the Christmas lights. The cold, thick, plastic wire wrapped around his throat. 'Ullk!'

Billy's fall came to a sudden halt, two storeys off the ground, legs kicking, jerking on the end of the electrical cable. Twisting. Spinning.

His chubby fingers clawed at the folds of fat on his neck. Can't breathe. . . Get the wire off. . . Oh God, oh God, oh God. . . CAN'T BREATHE.

White lights sparkled all around him, the bulbs breaking under his fingers, slashing his skin, leaving it slick with blood as he twisted and struggled.

And struggled.

And struggled.

And. . .

The last thing he saw before everything went black was the pear tree at sunset, hanging in an oak, lit by Christmas lights. Still beautiful.

2: Turtle Doves

A Christmas tree lurked in the corner of Oldcastle City Mortuary. Just a cheap artificial one – covered with brightly-coloured tinsel, blinking lights, and little plastic angels – but it lent the dissecting room a slightly festive air. They'd even managed to find a big star for the top of the tree: a nodding Elvis doll that twitched and lolled every time a refrigerator drawer slammed shut. All shook up.

It wasn't exactly Santa's grotto, but at least they'd made the effort.

Sandra leaned back against the sink, mobile phone jammed between her ear and shoulder, eating a Chicken-and-Mushroom Pot Noodle. 'Kevin? Hello? You there?' Pause two, three, four. 'Pick up, OK? Kevin?' The answering machine went bleep. She glanced at the pale mass of flesh on the cutting table, body cavity hollowed out and empty. 'Kevin? I'm gonna be late, OK? We're up to our ears in some fat bastard got himself hanged. I won't be round till later.' Sandra shovelled a forkful of noodles

12

into her mouth and mumbled her goodbyes. 'Love you.'
Then hung up.

She was just sooking the last of the juice from the
carton when Professor Muir muttered his way back from
the toilets. He took one look at her and sighed. 'I wish
you wouldn't eat those things in here: the smell upsets
Elvis.' He pointed at the King, who jiggled and nodded
his agreement as the mortuary door banged shut.

'I'm finished anyway.' She tossed the empty container
in the bin and pulled on a fresh pair of latex gloves. 'You
want me to do the spine?'

'Please.' Professor Muir went back to the mounds of
offal piled up on the gurney next to the cutting table.

Sandra pulled out the bone saw.

Click and the vacuum *whummmmmed* into action, ready
to whisk away any particles of blood and bone. Another
click and the saw whined into life, the vibrating blade
making her fingers tingle. 'You want the chord on its
own, or attached to the brain?'

'Surprise me.'

She smiled behind her mask – that was a challenge.
With all the insides scooped out, the body cavity was a
purple-and-red void, lined with shorn ribs where Sandra
had popped his ribcage off like the bonnet of a car. He
was a huge fat bastard, so big she could almost crawl
inside and pull the lid back on. The perfect hiding place.
Who'd look?

Grinning, she went to work on his spine, making the
saw shriek.

She was bagging up the internal organs when the phone
went: Oldcastle Force Headquarters, letting her know

13

another pair of bodies were on the way. She slammed the phone down. 'Arrrgh. . . It's the same thing every sodding Christmas.'

Professor Muir looked up from his preliminary report. 'Let me guess: suicide?'

'*Two* of them. Antisocial bastards.' She slipped the guy's lower intestine into a clear plastic pouch, sealed it, then hurled it into the open body cavity. 'Like we've got nothing better to do than piss about here dissecting them. *Some* of us had plans for tonight!'

'Don't sweat it. We'll process the paperwork tonight and carve them tomorrow. Consider it a Christmas bonus.'

Sandra stuffed the last of the bags into place, jammed the ribcage back on, then rolled the fatty skin back over the top, sewing it up with angry blanket stitches. She checked the clock on the wall: Six fifteen. She was already late, and two sets of paperwork were only going to make it worse.

Elvis danced for her as she wrestled the body back onto its refrigerated shelf and slammed the stainless steel door shut. She grabbed her mobile and stomped off to the viewing room to call Kevin, away from the professor's big hairy ears.

The little room was practically empty: just her; a vase full of artificial lilies; and the table they stuck dead bodies on. The families would troop into the soundproofed room opposite, look through the curtained window at what was left of their loved one, cry a bit. . . Then someone would say, 'Sorry for your loss' and the dearly departed would be wheeled away so Professor Muir could gut them like a fish. All very tasteful.

'Kevin?'

The telltale *click-hissssss* of the answering machine picking up, then it went into its pre-recorded routine: Kevin singing a bit of Pink Floyd's 'Comfortably Numb', only with different words. Asking her to leave a message. *'Bleeeeeeeeeeeeeeeeeeeeeeeeeep. . .'*

'Kevin? Look I know I'm late, but I'll make it up to you, OK? Ewan's pulling a green shift, so I'm yours *all* night. Better make sure you've got some baby oil in, 'cause I've got a surprise for. . .' A clunk on the line. 'Kevin? Kevin, is that you?' And then a metallic voice thanked her for calling, and hung up. 'Shite.'

Maybe he'd gone out? Flounced off in a huff because she was late? No, Kevin wouldn't do that to her, not when she'd blown forty quid on a kinky French maid's outfit from the Naughty Knicker Shop on Barnston Street at lunchtime. He'd *definitely* want to be around for that.

She stuck the mobile back in her pocket, rearranged her underwear, looked up. And nearly wet herself. There was a man on the other side of the observation window, staring in at her. . .

Christ sake: it was Ewan with his face pressed up against the glass, leering. She slammed her hand against the window, making him flinch back. 'You scared the life out of me!'

He was wearing a yellow high-viz jacket over the top of his police uniform, the peaked cap speckled with rain-drops. Not bad looking in a thin, George Clooney kind of way. Well, George Clooney crossed with John Cleese. He grinned like an idiot, mouthing something dirty at her through the glass, even though he knew the room was soundproofed.

She marched back into the cutting room.

15

DI 'Stinky' McClain – a hairy wee man with a face like a used condom – stood with his back to the wall of refrigerated drawers, sharing a joke with Professor Muir. 'So the receptionist pulls up her knickers and says, "It's *never* done that before!"' He laughed, jowls jiggling. '"It's never done that before." Get it?' Then waved at a tall, old, grave-looking man from the local funeral directors. 'Come on, Unwin, haven't got all night.'

Mr Unwin raised an eyebrow as he wheeled a stainless steel coffin in from the loading bay. 'Patience is a virtue, Inspector. The dead will not be rushed.' He activated the trolley's brake with a shiny black shoe, then headed back out for the other body.

This would be their double suicide then.

Sandra followed the undertaker out into the hallway.

Ewan was leaning against the wall, waiting for her. He grabbed her, planting a big wet kiss right on her mouth. 'What you still doing here? Thought you'd be home with Emma by now.'

Heat bloomed across Sandra's cheeks. She pulled herself free. 'Mum's looking after her. And I'd be home by now if it wasn't for you and your bloody suicides.'

He shrugged. 'Yeah, well, that's Christmas for you. Listen, I was thinking. . .' He grabbed her again, wrapping his hands around her buttocks. 'If you've got nothing on for the next fifteen minutes, maybe we could find a nice quiet room and—'

'No you bloody don't! Randy sod.' She backed away. 'You and your gonads can. . .'

Mr Unwin reappeared in the hallway, the wheels on his gurney squeaking as he pushed it through into the cutting room.

16

'Look, I got to go, OK? Sooner we get started on this pair, the sooner I get home.'

A playful smile sneaked its way onto his face. 'Maybe when *I* get home. . .?' Ever the optimist.

'Fat chance! Some of us have to get up for work in the morning.'

The smile vanished. 'How's Emma ever going to get a baby brother if we never do it? I could dress up: would that help? You know, be a fireman, or a doctor, or something?'

Change the subject. 'So, what we got – pair of oldies?'

'Naw.' He took her hand and led her back towards the dissecting room, where Professor Muir and Mr Unwin were hefting a dark-blue body-bag onto one of the mortuary's examination tables. 'Quite romantic really: man and woman, both early twenties, found holding hands on the bed. Painkillers, sleeping pills, and a big bottle of milk.'

'What the hell's romantic about that?'

'Decided they just couldn't live without each other. If one of them was going to die, they were *both* going to die.'

'Oh yeah?'

Professor Muir unzipped the bag, revealing a pretty blonde woman. Upturned nose, small overbite and bright-red lips. Her face was plastered with make-up, hiding the bloodless yellow waxy pall of death. But from the neck down she was all corpse. And not a natural blonde either.

'So which one was dying? Let me guess, she—'

'It was him. We found a letter from the hospital: test results. Turns out his HIV just got upgraded to full-blown AIDS.'

17

She scowled. 'Great, just what we need – a pair of fucking biohazards. They take *forever*.'

'Yeah, well, you just make sure you take care, OK?' He patted her on the arse. 'Don't want nothing happening to my woman.'

She didn't bother answering that, just stomped across the room as Muir and the undertaker manhandled the other body-bag out of its stainless steel coffin. 'Better watch out,' she pointed at the bag, 'this one's got AIDS.'

The professor swore, then pulled on a surgical mask and another pair of latex gloves. Scowled in DI 'Stinky' McClain's direction. 'No one bloody tells me anything.' He hauled down the zip, *zwwwwwwwwwwwip* . . . and there was Kevin.

The floor wobbled beneath Sandra's feet.

It was Kevin. Kevin was dead. Kevin was lying on his back, on a cutting slab, staring up at the mortuary ceiling with a faraway look in his glassy eyes.

She stumbled back a couple of steps. He had AIDS! Just two days ago they'd had unprotected sex in a 'dangerous area': the multi-storey car park behind Marks and Spencer. The bastard never even told her he was HIV positive!

Oh fuck. . .

'Sandra?' Good old Ewan, at her side in a flash, playing the big, strong husband. 'You OK?'

She couldn't take her eyes off Kevin's dead face.

The cheating, dirty, diseased, two-timing bastard hadn't even bothered to tell her! That could be *her* lying there next to him, all peaceful and serene and not having to worry about dying from some horrific disease. Instead of some STUPID BLONDE TART.

18

'Sandra?'

Kevin didn't even have the common decency to ask her to commit suicide with him. He never really loved her at all.

Men were such bastards.

3: French Hens

Marguerite Dumond could swear fluently in four languages, but right now she was practising her English. Clutching the side of her head, trying to staunch the bleeding. Leaning against the alley wall, as Philippe – still dressed in his chef's whites – kicked the shit out of the man who'd hit her.

Philippe's words were slurred, his heavy French accent rendered almost unintelligible by half a bottle of vodka on top of a hit of heroin, but his aim was dead on. 'How,' kick, 'many,' kick, 'times,' kick, 'do I have to tell you?' Kick. 'NEVER come around my work!' He took three steps back, had a run up, and slammed another boot into the man lying curled up on the alley floor. Then started stomping on his face.

Marguerite peeled the tea towel off her head. It was soaked through – glistening and dark red. The alleyway began to spin, her knees gave out – she sat down heavily on a crate full of empty bottles, making them rattle and clink. She wasn't going to be sick, she wasn't going to be

. . . oh yes she was. Marguerite leaned sideways and retched, spattering the cobbles with *coq au vin* and *crème brûlée*.

Philippe knelt on the man's chest and grabbed a handful of hair. Pulled his head off the ground. 'I ask you nicely!' A muffled grunt, then the hard, wet thunk of something being bounced off the alley floor. 'I ask you nicely, but you don't listen! You just,' thunk, 'don't,' thunk, 'listen.' Thunk. There was a moment's silence, then, 'You are stupid fucker, Kenny. You don't deserve friend like me. . .'

Marguerite raised her head, mouth coated with bitter slime.

Philippe was rummaging through Kenny's pockets, pulling out little silver foil packets. Then he settled back on his haunches and forced Kenny's mouth open.

'If you kill my waitress, how can she serve my food? A great restaurant, she cannot function without her front of house staff!' He ripped the end off a wrapper of heroin and poured it into Kenny's blood-smeared mouth. Then another and another and another. . . '*Bon appétit.*' He slammed his hand into Kenny's chest and the battered man convulsed, sending a plume of white powder up into the cold evening air.

Philippe clamped a hand over Kenny's mouth. 'I said, *Bon appétit!*'

And that was when Marguerite blacked out.

Half past seven in the morning and Alexander Garvie stood at the front door of *La Poule Française*, signing for the day's fish delivery – haddock, brill, turbot and hake. No sea bass, which would piss the chef off, but some days you just had to go with what was available.

He shuffled back in through the restaurant doors, heading

for the kitchen. If the reservations book was anything to go by, it'd be another busy day. Nearly full for lunch and packed for dinner. If it kept up like this they'd have to get more staff. Maybe a bigger restaurant?

Alexander shouldered his way through the kitchen doors and marched up to the walk-in fridge. There was a lot to be said for opening a new place: maybe something down by the river, or the cathedral?

He balanced the box of fish on his hip and cracked the fridge open.

It'd be expensive, but if they could match the success of *La Poule Française* they'd break even in about a year and a half. Eighteen months. It would be tight, but—

What the hell was that?

There was a man in the fridge!

He was lying flat on his back, next to the carrots and shallots, legs bent outwards, arms above his head. Like a frog waiting to be dissected.

'Hello?' Alexander slid the box onto the nearest shelf. 'You shouldn't be in here – it's not hygienic. . .'

The man didn't move.

'Are you OK?' He flicked on the inner light, breath misting around his head.

The man was *not* OK. His skin was the colour of rancid butter, spattered with dark-brown blood, and his forehead had a decided dip in it. Alexander reached out and touched the icy skin with trembling fingers. The man would never be OK ever again. He was dead.

'Oh dear God. . .' The first big glass of cognac hadn't settled his nerves and neither had the second one. The third was making things a little fuzzy around the edges, though. Alexander sat at the restaurant bar, trembling, drinking the good cognac, and staring at his mobile phone.

He should call the police.

Just as soon as he felt able to speak.

Call the police and tell them about the dead man in his fridge. And after that he might as well put a big GOING OUT OF BUSINESS sign in the window. Who wanted to eat in a restaurant with a corpse in the kitchen? They were ruined.

The sound of stainless steel platters clanging on the tiled floor came through from the kitchen, followed by French swearing. Philippe was in. His creased face appeared through the doors two minutes later – pink eyes, pale skin, dark-purple bags under the eyes. 'Mon Dieu. . . I feel like *merde.*' He rubbed a hand across his stubble-coated chin. 'Is that brandy or whisky?' pointing at the balloon glass in Alexander's hand.

'Er. . . Cognac.'

'Thank God.' He poured himself a huge measure, knocked it back in one gulp, refilled his glass, then let his head sink onto the bar. 'Please – when hangover kills me, don't let the bastards bury me in Paris. You know we've got a full service today?'

Alexander stood, levered Philippe off the bar and dragged him back into the kitchen. Propped him against the wall, and opened the fridge. The dead man stared up at them.

Philippe pursed his lips, frowned, looked at his glass of cognac, then frowned some more. 'Is this today's special? Because I thought we were doing seared sea bass with langoustine butter and *pommes dauphinoise.*'

'They didn't have any sea bass.'

23

Philippe shrugged. 'So you got me a dead body instead?'

'I DIDN'T GET HIM! He was here when I arrived.' Alexander slammed the fridge shut. 'What are we going to do? It'll be in all the papers; as soon as people find out we've got a corpse in here they'll cancel their reservations; we'll have to shut!' Getting louder and louder until Philippe grabbed him by the shoulders.

'Stop! Too loud! You're hurting my head.'

'What are we going to do? Where did he come from? We're ruined!'

Philippe let go, then opened the fridge again, staring in at the man on the floor. '*Merde*. . .' He buried his head in his hands. Groaned. Swore. 'We have to get rid of the body.'

Silence, broken only by the whurrrrrr of the fridge, trying to compensate for the door being open. 'No. We have to call the police.'

Philippe snorted. 'And then what? They'll close us down. *Martin White* is coming in tonight!'

'Oh God. . .' Martin White – food critic for the *Oldcastle News and Post*. A man who could make, or break, a restaurant with a single review. 'We're doomed.'

'No we're not. We get rid of the body and no one will know. Everything is the same. Nothing changes.'

'But . . . but. . .' Alexander closed the fridge door, unable to look at that battered face any longer. 'But how did he get here?'

Philippe licked his lips, cleared his throat, then laid a hand on Alexander's shoulder. 'Does it matter? He's here. We must get rid of him or the restaurant is finished.' Philippe turned a bleary eye on the kitchen, nodded, pulled on a heavy apron, and unrolled his bundle of knives. Picked out a boning knife and a long metal steel. 'We cut him up.' The blade made shnick, shnick, shnick noises as he sharpened it.

Alexander drained his cognac and nodded. It made sense. Cut him up. Cut him up into little pieces. 'Then what?'

'Then?' Philippe tested the knife's edge. 'We get rid of him.'

'But someone will find the pieces!'

A frown, then a smile. 'We will mince the meat, yes? Cook it off and throw it out in the bins. Looks like any other mince. No one will know.'

'Mince. . .? Yes, mince. . .' sweat prickled between Alexander's shoulder blades. Maybe another drink to steady his nerves?

Philippe pulled out a meat cleaver and a hacksaw. 'Now, you help me get him up on the worktop, then you lock all the doors and make sure no one comes in here.'

'But the veg man—'

'No one! Take the deliveries out front. I don't care! But not in here!' He clicked on the radio, cranking up the volume. Then they hauled the dead man out of the fridge. And got to work.

Lunchtime was packed and it didn't help that Marguerite hadn't turned up for work that morning, so they were a waitress down. Alexander pushed through from the dining room with an order for veal escalope, *coq au vin*, and turbot with champagne hollandaise.

The kitchen was a well-oiled machine, and so was Philippe. He'd downed at *least* half a bottle of cognac this morning – while he was cutting and mincing and frying – before moving on to vodka-and-tonic. And now he was drinking ice-cold beer, directing the sous chef, pastry chef, dish washer, and waitresses, turning out food that was the talk of Oldcastle.

It was as if nothing had ever happened.

When the lunchtime rush was over, Philippe and Alexander sat in the cramped manager's office, drinking strong cups of coffee with the door closed. The chef leaned back in his seat and groaned at the ceiling tiles.

Alexander fiddled with his mug. 'Erm. . . How are we getting on with . . . with our visitor?'

A shrug. 'He's in bags at the back of the fridge. Looks just like fried mince.' Another groan and Philippe slumped forwards. 'The trouble is the bones.'

'Oh God.' The bones – a whole human skeleton would look suspicious, even in a restaurant's rubbish. 'We're ruined! We're—'

Philippe held up a hand. 'No, not ruined. I chopped the bones, put them in the oven. They'll roast and dry out. We smash them with a hammer into little pieces. Then we dump them. Not a problem.'

'What about the . . . the. . .' Alexander tapped the side of his head.

'Meh. . .' Philippe finished his coffee. 'When you hack a man's skull into eight pieces with a cleaver, it looks like any other bones. No one will notice. Trust me. It is all good again.'

Alexander tried for a smile, and managed to find one. They were in the clear – the body was taken care of, the lunchtime rush was over. Now all they had to do was impress the socks off Martin White and everything was perfect. 'Philippe, I want you to get some sleep, OK? The staff can take care of the clean-down and prep for the evening sitting. You rest. I want you at your best when Martin White gets here.' The smile turned into a beam.

Everything was going to be all right.

Philippe looked a lot better when he emerged at half past six: wide awake and smiling. The white powder on his top lip was probably just flour, wasn't it? He'd been making bread, or pastry, or checking the . . . something. That was all. Nothing else.

Alexander opened the reservations book, then closed it again. Lined it up with the edge of the bar. Took a deep breath. Only two people had a key to the restaurant: him and Philippe, and he *certainly* hadn't stuck a dead body in the fridge, so it had to be Philippe. But. . . But Philippe was a brilliant chef, you had to expect a certain amount of eccentric behaviour from geniuses. And besides, where was Alexander going to get anyone else as talented in Oldcastle?

So they would carry on as if nothing had ever happened. They would get their good review and open up a second restaurant, *Le Coq Rouge* – it would become a beacon of French cuisine for all of Oldcastle to see. No: all of Scotland! It would win three Michelin stars. And all because Alexander had the wisdom to not call the police.

Marguerite had even turned up for work – albeit seven hours late – with a patch of white gauze taped to the back of her head and a story about being mugged. She shared some knowing glances with Philippe, but. . . But it was probably nothing. It would be fine. Everything was going to be OK.

* * *

27

At ten to seven, Alexander gathered the staff together in the dining room and gave them a pep talk: Martin White was coming in tonight; they were not to be nervous; they were a professional team; they were the best French restaurant in the whole city; do their best and tonight would be perfect!

And then he went back to the manager's office to chew his fingernails and watch the clock. Counting the minutes until Martin White's reservation for one, at eight o'clock.

'Well?' Alexander shifted from foot to foot on the tiled kitchen floor.

Philippe tossed a handful of langoustine tails into hot garlic and herb butter. 'It's a crime we have no sea bass, but—'

'What's he ordered?'

Philippe gave the pan one last flick, then poured the langoustines over a fillet of turbot resting on a bed of mashed butter beans with salsa verde. 'Soup, paté and crevettes to start with, then the veal, entrecote, turbot and lamb.' He wiped the edge of the plate and dressed it with a sprinkle of finely chopped chives. 'Service!'

'Good, good. . .'

Marguerite appeared and whisked the plate away into the restaurant.

Alexander glanced at the fridge. 'And what about . . . you know . . . that thing?'

'I had Colin throw half the mince in the bin when he came on. Told him it was rancid.'

'Excellent. Yes, that's good. Fine.' He wrung his hands, smiled, fidgeted. Then went to stand at the door, looking out through the glass porthole at the dining room, searching the faces until he found the bane of every restaurateur's life. Martin White: flabby, pale, with a shock of dyed-black hair, sitting on his own at a table big enough for four. Marguerite offering him the first taste from a bottle of wine, checking to make sure it was acceptable. White's face clouded over as he swilled the liquid back and forth, then spat it out into another glass and complained bitterly.

'Oh God. . .' Alexander bit his bottom lip hard enough to draw blood. Things were starting to go sour.

Half an hour later and White was picking at his main courses. Starting with the lamb, then dipping into the other dishes. Making snide comments into a Dictaphone.

Marguerite stormed through from the dining room, burst into tears, went straight into the walk-in fridge, slammed the door, and screamed.

It took Alexander five minutes to coax her out.

'He's being such a bastard.' She slumped back against the pass, wiping her eyes with a dishtowel. 'The wine's too warm, the wine's too cold, the salt's too salty, the soup's too wet, the candles don't smell nice. . .' And then she started swearing in French, but Alexander wasn't listening. He was peering out through the porthole at the man who was going to ruin his restaurant.

'Merde!'

Oh God, what now?

Philippe was on his knees in front of one of the ovens. Staring in at the empty space.

'What? What's gone wrong?' *Everything* was going wrong!

'The. . .' Philippe checked the empty oven again. 'He. . . They're gone.'

29

'What are gone? Philippe: what's gone?'

'The bones.' Philippe slammed the oven door and stood, eyes raking across the kitchen. 'Angus!'

The commis chef flinched, nearly dicing his fingers along with the celeriac. 'Yes, chef?' Standing to attention.

'Bones – in this oven. Where?'

A smile broke across Angus's face, and he sagged a little. 'I made stock, chef.' He pointed at the huge pot sitting on the hob at the back of the kitchen – the cooker reserved for boiling bones, vegetables and off-cuts. 'Onion, carrot, celery, peppercorns, bay leaf, thyme. . .' The smile slipped a bit. 'Something wrong, chef?'

Philippe opened his mouth, but the only thing to come out was a small squeak.

'Chef?'

'Did. . . Are we using it?'

Angus frowned, as if Philippe had just insulted his mother. '*Yes*, chef: it's good veal stock.'

Alexander stared at the big pot bubbling away, then at the soup, and the sauces and everything else 'veal' stock ended up in. Even the fish. They were ruined! 'I—'

'Good!' Philippe managed to plaster on a smile. 'Er . . . well done.'

'Thank you, chef.'

It was time for more brandy.

After dessert, Martin White started in on the liqueurs and whiskies. Getting louder and more obnoxious with every drink. One by one, the other tables drifted away, until it was quarter past eleven and the place was empty. Apart from Mr White.

He was probably planning on skipping out without

paying as well. Expecting *La Poule Française* to pick up the tab in a last-ditch attempt to curry favour and get a good review. Well, if that was what it would take. . .

'We should have thrown him out!' Philippe stood at Alexander's shoulder, glaring through the porthole at Martin White. 'Go find a McDonald's, you fat *connard*.'

The kitchen was deserted – Alexander had sent everyone home once the washing up was done. Well, there was no point everyone hanging around getting depressed, waiting for Martin White to put them out of business. So now it was just the two of them out back and Marguerite out front; gritting her teeth and serving the horrible Mr White.

'We're ruined. . .'

'Fat pig doesn't deserve to eat my food!'

'He'll give us a terrible review. . .'

'I should have pissed in his soup.' Philippe threw his hands in the air. 'Fuck him. I'm going to get drunk.' He grabbed his coat and stormed out the back door, slamming it behind him.

There was a flurry of movement in the dining room: White was getting to his feet, preparing to leave.

Alexander straightened his jacket, plastered on his best smile, and went through to meet him. Give it one last shot. Save the restaurant. Even if it meant grovelling and paying for White's meal.

He got Marguerite to fetch the reviewer's coat then told her she could knock off for the night. At least this way she wouldn't see him humiliating himself, bowing and scraping.

'Mr White!' He beamed, holding his hands out as if they were old friends. 'How lovely of you to have joined us. I hope you enjoyed your meal?'

White sneered back at him. His voice was slightly slurred by three bottles of vintage Bordeaux. 'You can hope.'

There was an awkward silence, broken only by the bell above the door as Marguerite made good her escape.

'Perhaps. . .' Alexander picked a napkin off the table, fidgeted with it, sweating, smiling for all he was worth. 'Perhaps I can treat you to a fine cognac? It's a 1936 Louis XIII Grande Champagne: quite exquisite. . .?' And very expensive. But the restaurant was worth it.

Philippe was the first one into work on Friday morning. Head pounding, eyes like devilled eggs, mouth like the bottom of the grease trap. That's what he got for gulping down tequila and snorting coke at the Bain-Marie in Logansferry till four that morning. Bragging to all his chef friends about the exquisite meal he'd just served up to Martin White.

And it *was* an exquisite meal, each course more perfect than the last.

White wouldn't know fine dining if it crawled up his trouser leg and bit him on the *derriere*.

The review would be in the paper tomorrow. Soon people would start cancelling their bookings – he'd seen it happen time and time again. The only place that consistently got a good review from White was Fandingo's on Crenton Lane, and why? Because they had a waiter called Dave suck the fat pig's cock under the table while he ate, *that's* why.

Philippe cracked open the fridge. Time to throw the last bags of Kenny into the garbage – let the bin men take care of him. And there, lying on his back in the middle of the tiles, was Martin White. Pasty faced and stiff as a board.

With a small smile, Philippe unrolled his knives and started carving.

4: Calling Birds

Agnes is in the full throws of simulated orgasm when Tracy finally gets someone to answer their damn phone. The word '*Hello?*' pops into her earpiece.

'Can I speak to the home owner?' Ignoring the cries of 'Yes! Yes! Oh GOD YES!!!' coming from the next cubicle along.

'*Why?*'

'I'm calling from PVSafe solutions: if you could replace all the windows in your house for free, how many would you replace?'

'*Oh for goodness sake: I was in the bloody bath! BUGGER OFF!*' The clatter of a phone being slammed down, then the indifferent '*burrrrrr*' of an open line.

Tracy groans, unplugs her headset and levers herself out of her seat. Bladder's killing her. Correction: the baby's foot in her bladder is killing her. At forty-one weeks pregnant she looks like she's swallowed a sofa and feels like it too. She picks a wedge of floral-print maternity dress from between her buttocks. Very classy.

She waddles over to Mr Aziz, who sits at a desk by the door squinting at a copy of the *Racing Post*. Picking the horses he's going to lose money on tomorrow.

Tracy holds out her hand. 'Pee break.'

He doesn't even look up at her. 'Again?'

'Yes, *again*.'

He shrugs and passes her the bathroom key. She only gets paid for the calls she makes, so who cares if she spends half the evening in the toilets? Five minutes later she's standing at the coffee machine, crunching away on a handful of antacid tablets, waiting for her camomile tea to infuse, sniffing the heady aroma of percolator coffee and wishing to God this damn baby would hurry up so she can get back to proper drinks again. Got enough on her plate without having to give up caffeine and alcohol too. She nods as Agnes limps over. 'How's it going?'

The old lady grins, exposing a perfect set of brand-new dentures. 'Twenty-one so far.' Agnes leans forward, voice dropping to a theatrical whisper. 'I'm gonnae get Mr McWhirter one of them cashmere cardigans from Markies.' She pats her rock-solid blue-rinsed hairdo. 'And maybe get myself a new hat, from Santa. What about you, dear? How you holdin' up?'

Tracy shrugs. 'Been better.' She tries for a smile – risky, because the tears were never far away. *Especially* when someone offered sympathy. 'Chloe's missing her granny, dad's distraught, and John's lost his job. . .' Right on cue her eyes fill up. 'I'm sorry,' She sniffs, running a hand over her puffy face. 'Bloody hormones aren't helping.'

Agnes doesn't say anything, just envelops her in a hug that smells of Parma Violets, Mint Imperials and stale cigarettes. 'You should go home.'

'I . . . I can't.' Tracy pulls a tatty hanky from her sleeve and blows her nose. 'We need the money for Mum's funeral.' Sniff.

Agnes looks back at the row of cubicles. 'Tell you what, I'm doin' fine this month: why don't you take over my phone for a bit? Be "Sexy Sadie" for a while. Easy money. . . Aye as long as you don't mind all the screaming.' She winks. 'Nothing like it to get your knickers waggin', though. Soon as you get home you'll be tearing the pants off that husband of yours.'

Tracy pats her swollen midriff. 'That's how I got into trouble in the first place.'

Tracy shifts in her seat. Bloody haemorrhoids are worse than the hormones. Can't get Agnes's headset to sit properly either – keeps digging into her ear. 'I've got your big hard dick in my mouth and I'm sucking like. . .' She stares into space for a moment. 'Like a vacuum cleaner!'

'*Unnngh, unnnngh, ungggh. . .*' From the other end of the phone.

'God you're so big!' There's something very liberating about having pretend sex on the phone with strangers. Saying things she'd never *dream* of saying to John. 'Oh, yes, like that: I love it when you bite my arse!'

'*Unnnngh, unnnnngh, unnnnnnnngh!*'

'Come on my tits!'

'*Unnnnnnnnnnnnnnnnnnngh!*' Pant, pant, pant. '*Oh God. . .*' Sigh.

Tracy checks the timer – three minutes fifteen seconds. The quickest one yet. For a moment she almost tells him not to worry, it happens to all men at some point, but that's probably not what Mr Heavy Breathing wants to hear. So she settles for, 'Oh, you were soooo good! I'm rubbing your spunk all over my big firm breasts.' A little more post-coital smut brings the call up to six and a half minutes.

'You know, Dear,' Agnes leans on the cubicle wall, half-moon spectacles balanced on the end of her nose, 'you need to slow them *down* a bit. As soon as they. . . You know. . .' She makes a euphemistic hand gesture, which is ironic considering she's spent most of the evening telling complete strangers to fuck her harder. 'Once they've "finished": they hang up, and you stop getting paid. Don't go straight for the mince and tatties – tease them. You'll make a lot more money.' She looks left and right, like she's about to impart a trade secret. 'I always do this big long striptease – they love it.'

'Striptease is it?' Daphne McCafferty pokes her head over from the cubicle opposite. 'I likes to touch myself all over. Gets them all hot and bothered, and it takes forever when you're my size!' She laughs, throwing her head back, making her chins wobble. Daphne McCafferty – AKA: Naughty Nikki – sixty-three next April.

The only one not offering up any advice is 'Busty Becky', a granny from Dundee with an artificial hip, white hair and a big hairy mole on her chin. She just sits there, clickity-clacking away – moaning into her headset and knitting at the same time. Making a big woolly jumper with reindeer on it, while someone wanks into her ear on a premium-rate phonecall. 'Ooh, it's so big!' Knit one, pearl one. 'You know you want it. Beg for it. Get on your hands and knees and *beg*.'

Mr Aziz comes over to see what all the standing around is in aid of. 'What?' He's got his hands in the pockets of

37

his cardigan, stretching it all out of shape. 'Why am I not hearing the sounds of hot passion?'

Agnes slaps him on the back, making him lose his balance. 'We're just impartin' the tricks of the trade to young Tracy here, aren't we Daphne?'

'Aye,' Daphne grins, 'we're gonnae turn her intae a top-flight phone-sex girl. Like in that movie with Rex Harrison and the old geezer.' Her grin turned into a frown. 'Oh, what's it called. . . You know, the one with '"I'm gettin' married in the mornin'"'. . .'

She launches into the song and Agnes joins in, all merry and jolly until 'Busty Becky' stands, one hand clamped over her mouthpiece. 'Will you lot keep it down? I'm trying to bugger a solicitor called Steve from Castleview, and he's a bit flighty about the size of my strap-on.'

The singing dissolves into grins and sighs, then everyone goes back to their phones. Everyone except for Agnes and Tracy.

Mr Aziz frowns at her. 'How come you're on the Sexy Sadie line, then? I mean, no offence, but I think you're a bit young for the phone sex business.'

'I need the money, it's my mother's—'

'Look, Tracy,' Mr Aziz lays a hand on her shoulder, 'I like you and I understand that you've got problems, but my customers expect a certain level of service when they phone up. They—'

'Hoy!' Agnes pokes him in the chest. 'Now you listen to me, Kamuzu Aziz, that poor girl can talk dirty with the rest of them. *And* she needs the money.'

'But—'

'But nothin'. If you think. . .' She stared into the cubicle: the Sexy Sadie hotline was ringing. 'Well, go on then, Tracy – show him what you're made of!'

She does, making a big show of the striptease and self-fondling. The man on the other end moans and groans and grunts his way to fifteen minutes forty-nine seconds, Tracy's longest romantic encounter all night by a long shot. She hangs up and beams. Agnes gives her a round of applause.

Mr Aziz shrugs. 'All right, all right. You can be Sexy Sadie for the rest of the night. Only put more *moaning* into it. The punters like a bit of moaning.' Then he shuffles back to his copy of the *Racing Post*.

Tracy blinks back the tears. 'Thanks, Agnes.'

'Don't mention it. Now, if you'll excuse me, I've got some dodgy double glazin' to sell.'

Now she's learned the magic formula, there's no stopping her. The next call lasts twenty minutes and the one after that a full twenty-five. Do this every night and their money worries would be over. Well, not *over*, but they'd be able to pay off the funeral.

Maybe Mr Aziz could put her on full time? She could be 'Spanking Susan', or 'Horny Helen', or 'Lusty Laura', or something. Have explicit postcards of her very own plastered over every telephone box in Oldcastle. Not that she'll pose for the photo herself – it'll be months before she loses the baby weight, and let's face it, she was hardly skinny to start with – no she'd do the same as all the other women and let Mr Aziz pick one of his 'nieces' to model the thong and stilettos.

The next call is a funny one, and not funny 'ha, ha' either. It's a woman with a growling, furious voice. '*I know what you are! I know what you are!'* A nut job, phoning up to cause trouble, too stupid to realize that she's getting charged for every second the call lasts, just like the men who want someone to talk filthy to them. *'And I know* where *you are!'*

Tracy blinks. 'Excuse me?'

'You heard! I've got a friend in the police: they traced the number. I know where you are, whore! You're a shit stain on the human race, you hear me, WHORE?' There's more, but Tracy doesn't listen to it, just kills the line and sits back shaking.

The phone goes again and she jumps, letting out a little shriek. No one notices: shrieks and moans are par for the course around here.

There's silence from the other end of the phone and then, *'Is that Sadie?'* A man's voice; not the mad harpy again. Thank God for that.

Maybe she should try out her new persona: Dirty Debbie?

No, better save it until she's got her own kinky postcards. Start to build a clientele.

'You better believe it.' She goes for deep and sultry, but it comes out sounding a bit blocked up instead. 'Do you like dirty girls?'

'You don't sound like Sadie. . . I want to speak to Sadie.' There's something familiar about his voice, but Tracy can't quite place it.

'I told you: I'm Sadie. If you're going to be naughty I'll have to spank you!'

'I don't. . .' Another pause: he's thinking about it. He has to be one of Agnes's regulars, or he wouldn't know what the real Sadie sounds like. *'I suppose I have been naughty.'*

40

'Hmmm, well I think we'll have to do something about that. Won't we?' She launches into her routine, doing the undressing thing while he whimpers and groans on the other end of the phone.

Where the hell does she know his voice from? It's so bloody familiar. . .

Then he says, *'Naughty! I'm a naughty boy! Spank me!'* and she knows. Oh God!

She punches the button and hangs up on him. The stopwatch has the call at a little under five minutes. She sits staring at the phone. It starts to ring again.

Go away, go away, go away!

Fifteen rings later, and Agnes is hanging over the side of the cubicle. 'Are you feeling all right, dear?' The phone keeps ringing. 'Is it the baby? Have you got your contractions?'

Tracy drags her eyes from the phone and looks up at her. 'No. . . Please, can. . . I can't . . . it's. . .' She pulls her headset off and backs away from the cubicle. Her stomach *churns* – like morning sickness all over again.

Agnes hurries around and takes the call, telling the man on the other end what he wants to hear.

It's stupid. She's imagining it. A lot of people sound the same over the phone – *especially* when they've got an Oldcastle accent.

Agnes moans and groans her way to a climax. Only takes ten minutes, she must be worried to end it so quickly. She disconnects the call. 'What is it, Tracy? You can tell me: what is it?'

She points at the phone and says, 'I . . . I thought it was. . .' She blushes, picks at a button on her maternity dress. 'Never mind.'

Agnes grins. 'I know what you mean. First couple of months I was *sure* I was speaking to my neighbour, milkman, the boy who works at the bingo hall on Thursdays. . . In the end I just decided, "So what?" They don't know I'm Sexy Sadie: doesn't matter if I recognize them, does it? It's all just make-believe.' Agnes gets up, then pats the vacant seat. 'Come on. Sooner you get back on the horse, the sooner you're earning again.'

Tracy nods. It's stupid.

She settles back into the seat.

Agnes hands her the headset. 'That was one of my biggest fans. Calls at least twice a week, poor soul. Wife won't let him touch her. If it wasn't for me, I don't know what he'd do.'

Tracy manages a sickly smile and doesn't tell Agnes why she thinks she knows the voice. Nor does she dial 1471 to find the number he phoned from. She just sits and stares at the phone, willing it to ring again and erase the last Caller ID record.

It was stupid. It wasn't him. Her dad wouldn't ring a sex line to masturbate down the phone at her, not while Mum's lying in a coffin at the funeral director's.

The phone rings and she nearly screams. With trembling fingers she puts on the headset, takes three deep breaths, and picks up the call.

Maybe selling double glazing isn't such a bad job after all.

5: Gold Rings

There is never a good time to look upon the face of a dead loved one. This is something Mr Unwin understands all too well, because he sees it every day.

Mrs Riley is the latest addition to his world: the world of mahogany caskets and heavy velvet curtains: of subdued lighting and soothing classical music. And the calming smell of lavender, to cover anything 'unpleasant' coming from the dearly departed.

Mrs Riley cries and cries and cries, while Mr Riley does his best to comfort his heavily pregnant wife. She is distraught: she has lost her mother. He is stoic: he has lost his mother-in-law, which is not the same thing at all. And little Chloe – who has lost her grandmother – seems completely unconcerned. She sits on the carpet by the casket, pulling the petals off a white carnation and sticking them up her nose.

And all the time Mr Unwin stands in silence by the door of the small room, hands folded in front of him, waiting for the family to finish. Patience is a virtue. The dead will not be rushed.

Finally, Mrs Riley cries herself to a shuddering standstill and her husband leads her from the chapel of rest, taking little Chloe with them. 'Thanks.' He places a hand on Mr Unwin's shoulder. 'You've done a wonderful job. She looks so. . .' He casts a glance back at the open coffin. 'So peaceful.'

Mr Unwin nods. 'I'm glad we could help.' And shows them to the door.

'Well?' Mr McNulty shifts his chair closer to the embalming table as Mr Unwin pushes back through into the preparation room. 'They gone?' He runs a thick-fingered hand across his shiny scalp, stroking the liver spots.

'Yes, Duncan, they've gone.' Mr Unwin takes off his black jacket and hangs it up, then dons the heavy rubber apron again. 'I'm sorry it took so long, but Mrs Riley was quite distraught.'

Mr McNulty shrugs, then takes another swig from his bottle of Glenfiddich, 'They say it?'

'"Very peaceful"? Yes, they said it.' They always say it.

'You going to make *her* look "very peaceful"?' He points at the large, doughy, naked woman on the embalming table. 'You going to. . .' Another drink. 'You going to. . .'

Mr Unwin folds his hands, stands still as a headstone. 'Are you sure you want to be here while I prepare her?'

But Mr McNulty doesn't reply, just stares at the pale, yellowy body.

'Duncan, please, I'll take good care of her, I promise. Go home and get some rest.'

'No. No I want to be with her. To help. It's the least I

can do. . .' He wipes his nose on his sleeve. 'I. . . Oh God. . .' And with that Mr McNulty dissolves into tears.

Mr Unwin waits until he has cried himself out, before escorting him to the back door. 'Don't worry, she's in good hands.'

Mr McNulty nods, wipes his eyes, then slouches back up the stairs.

Mr Unwin closes and locks the back door. Then turns and smiles at the woman lying in the preparation room waiting for him to work his magic.

Mrs McNulty was, and still is, a big woman: eighteen stone of flesh, bone and fat. All those years she and Mr McNulty have lived in the small flat above the funeral home – Unwin and McNulty, Undertakers est. 1965 – and this is the first time Mr Unwin has ever seen her naked.

He pats her pale belly. The skin is cold and greasy, like chicken taken from the refrigerator. But Mrs McNulty is no spring chicken. Then again, Mr McNulty isn't much of a catch either: short, chubby, bald and dour. But a good man for all that. . .

There is a *particular* smell that comes with embalming people. A mixture of raw meat and disinfectant, with a faint underlying taint of decay. It's an acquired taste, but Mr Unwin has had years to get used to it. Now it smells like home. Like a job well done. A chance to use his talents. To do what he was born to do. To make the dearly departed look peaceful.

And then, when Mrs McNulty's body fluids have been swapped out for preservative, and all her personal orifices bunged up with gauze pads to make sure she doesn't leak

45

in her casket, he pulls over his special toolkit and stares at her face. Studying the lines and wrinkles, the thread-veins in her cheeks, the mole on her chin with one long hair poking out, the freckles on her forehead. Then sets to work on her face.

It's a delicate job, one Mr Unwin has been doing since he was a small boy in his father's funeral home. He has the gift: layers and layers of flesh-pink, blended beauti-fully to a soft sheen on her sallow skin; a subtle red lipstick painted on glued-together lips; eye shadow and blusher; her grey hair carefully styled. When he's finished she looks better than she has for years.

Death suits Mrs McNulty. She should have died years ago.

Mr McNulty has provided his wife's favourite ensemble for her final journey – a blue, knee-length dress, a pair of thick brown tights, black pumps and a large leather handbag. It takes a while to dress the deceased, but Mr Unwin has had plenty of practice putting clothes on dead bodies. At last she's ready for her final journey.

It isn't easy, hefting his partner's wife into her coffin – walnut and maple with a pale-blue silk lining and genuine brass handles – but he manages. There's a reason people call it 'dead weight'. And Mrs McNulty has lots of it.

She looks so peaceful lying there, and Mr Unwin takes a moment to give thanks for her life, before wheeling her into the chapel of rest, where she'll spend the night with Mrs Riley's mother. A pair of old ladies, comfortable together in eternal sleep.

Now only one thing remains to be done.

Mr Unwin takes Mrs McNulty's hands and arranges

them across her chest, right over left, gluing them together to make sure they stay in place. Sometimes the dearly departed move in transit, or the change in temperature from the funeral home, to the hearse, to a cold and draughty church makes their tendons contract. It can be *very* distressing for the family, and contact adhesive covers up a multitude of sins.

Back in the front office, Mr Unwin settles behind his desk and looks out over the darkened rooftops of Oldcastle. Eight days to Christmas and there's not a single decoration or card up in the funeral home. This is not a place for celebration; it is a place for quiet respect and mourning.

There's a bottle of Highland Park in his desk and he pours himself a modest dram, adding a splash of cold water to loosen the whisky's aroma. He raises his glass to the sleeping city. 'To Mrs McNulty, may you have all the peace in death you denied your husband in life.' Which was why Mr McNulty had pushed her down the stairs, fracturing her skull and breaking her neck.

With a faint smile, Mr Unwin unlocks the drawer in his desk and pulls out a long wooden box. It opens with a small golden key – *click* – and its contents sparkle in the dim light. Wedding rings, large and small, new and old, all cut or pulled from the fingers of the dearly departed. He places Mrs McNulty's ring on the pile, admiring the way it fits so neatly with the others. All those lives. All that love. All that grief.

He has a separate box to keep the severed fingers in.

Contact adhesive covers a multitude of sins.

6: Geese a-Laying

Kathy Geddes didn't look in any fit state to do a runner – shuffling along, trying not to aggravate her piles and stitches – but that didn't mean she was free to wander round Castle Hill Infirmary unsupervised.

Val Macintyre dawdled along beside her, hands in the pockets of her uniform trousers. Of course she *could* have worn plain clothes, treated it as an undercover operation, but that was just asking for trouble. No, a prison officer wore a uniform for a reason – so everyone knew who was who. And besides, it wouldn't feel right: escorting a prisoner out of uniform. Not having that comforting bundle of keys jangling against her leg.

Geddes winced her way down the stairs, across the corridor and out into a small, bleak courtyard, lined on four sides with dirty brick and lichen-speckled concrete. The hospital had put up a bus shelter, smack bang in the middle, so patients could have a cigarette without setting off every smoke detector in the place.

A wheezy old man huddled in the smoking hut, drip

stand in one hand and a ratty-looking roll-up in the other.

Val waited for him to finish and hobble off before crossing her arms and squinting at Geddes. 'You shouldn't be smoking.'

'Bite me.' She took a deep drag on her cigarette and oozed smoke towards the ceiling.

'You're supposed to be breastfeeding!'

'Bugger that: little bastard's chewed me nipples raw. They're like half a pound of mince. He can go on the bottle.'

'Don't call him that.'

'What, "bastard"? Why not? That's what he is, isn't he? Haven't got a clue who his dad is.'

'I don't like it.' Val turned her back and stared out of the rain-flecked glass. At least they didn't have long to go. Thank *God*.

Behind her, Geddes was humming something vaguely recognizable as a Christmas carol. Not that there was much sign of the festive season in the smoking hut, just a big poster reminding everyone that SMOKING KILLS!

'When you going to get me some more vodka then?'

'You're supposed to be looking after that baby, not boozing it up.' She squared her shoulders and put on her prison guard voice. 'That's long enough. We're going back to the ward.'

'But I don't *want* to!' Whining and petulant. Like a child. 'I'm fed up of this shite!'

'You should have thought of that before you got pregnant, you selfish little. . .' Val rubbed a hand across her face. Took a deep breath. 'Sorry. I didn't mean that. It's been a long week.'

Geddes shrugged and headed back out into the rain.

* * *

Oldcastle Royal Infirmary sulked on the south-east corner of Castle Hill – the ancient building a testament to Victorian civic pride. The sort of place red brick and long, winding corridors went to die. Sometime in the late sixties the city council had added an extension: two massive wings in glass, steel and concrete.

The maternity ward was in the older part.

They'd put Kathy Geddes in a private room: somewhere secluded, where she wouldn't upset the other mothers with her convictions for assault, lewd behaviour, drunk and disorderly, soliciting, robbery, and the *pièce de résistance*: attempted murder.

She didn't deserve to have a baby. She was a terrible mother to the three kids she already had, never mind a new one – drinking, smoking, doing drugs. . . Not like Val. Val and her husband did everything they were supposed to, followed the doctor's instructions to the letter, but could *she* get pregnant? No. Geddes was like a bloody rabbit and Val couldn't even have one.

She sat in the uncomfortable visitor's chair and watched the cot while Geddes ate crisps and stared at the television.

'Rolf' – that was what she'd called her little baby boy. 'Rolf Ainsley Schofield Geddes.' She shouldn't be allowed to have children, torturing the poor kid like that.

It was obvious to anyone with half a brain that he wasn't a '*Rolf*'. He was a Brian, or a Donald. . . Yes, definitely a Donald.

He yawned, showing off a little pink mouth and tiny pink tongue. Donald Macintyre. It had a lovely ring to it. Donald Philip Macintyre. Philip after her father, who went to his grave without ever having a grandchild.

Geddes stuffed in another handful of crisps, chewing with her mouth open.

It just wasn't *fair*.

A nurse came round with the tea trolley at ten p.m., wearing brown felt antlers and novelty-snowmen earrings that flashed on and off. Geddes curled her top lip. 'Bloody tea tastes like warm pish. And how come you can't get any decent sodding biscuits on the NHS?'

The nurse ignored her, gave Val a cup of coffee and a long-suffering sigh, then disappeared off to spread cheer among the other mothers.

Now they were all alone: Geddes, Val and little Donald.

'Right,' Val put her empty cup down on the bedside cabinet, 'are you sure you're feeling up to this?'

'Bloody right I am.' Kathy levered herself out of bed. 'Driving me mad, sitting here all day.'

'What about the stitches?'

'Bugger the stitches.' She peeled off her hospital-issue nightie and stood there in a baggy bra and grey pants, stomach swollen and saggy at the same time. 'You going to help or not?'

Val nodded, took a deep breath, and helped Kathy into a brand-new set of clothes. Then stood back as she stared at herself in the mirror. 'Isn't that better?'

'Jesus. . .' Geddes pulled at the top Norman had picked up from the big Marks and Spencer on Dundas Road, 'Is your bloody husband blind? What the hell's this supposed to be?'

'You look fine.'

'I look like a bloody frump.'

Val stripped down to her underwear then clambered

51

into a pair of tan chinos and a pink sweatshirt, and pulled a baby sling on over the top. It still had the price tag from John Lewis dangling from one of the straps. She stuffed their discarded clothes and a few supplies into a large grey holdall. Nappies, cotton buds, surgical gloves, baby wipes, that kind of thing.

She handed Geddes a green Oldcastle Tigers baseball cap. 'Are you ready?'

'You'll have to carry the little bastard – my arse is giving me gyp.' Geddes peered out through the blinds at the corridor. 'You *sure* we'll no' be seen?'

'Come on darling, come to your aunty Val. . .' She lifted him out of his cot, wrapped him up in a snugly new blanket, then slipped him into the baby sling. Warmth spread through her like sunshine as she looked down at Donald's little pink face. He was perfect. Utterly, utterly *perfect*.

'You finished sodding about? 'Cos I'd like to get the hell out of here!'

Val pulled on a long overcoat, fastening it over Donald in his sling: hiding him from sight. Another baseball cap topped off her disguise. Not even her own mother would recognize her.

There was no one in the corridor, just the low gurgle and hum of the hospital's heating system to keep them company as they walked past the antenatal rooms, examination suite and birthing pool.

The nurses' station was empty – ten-past ten, right on schedule. The duty nurse would be away getting things organized for tomorrow's rounds. No witnesses.

They pushed out through the ward's outer doors, keeping their heads down to avoid the cameras.

Five minutes later they were outside in the crisp December air. Sunday night, one week before Christmas, and everything was going perfectly. . . Val stared out at the car park, then the road beyond the iron railings. The whole pace was deserted, no sign of Norman or the car.

Val checked her watch: ten twenty-one. 'We're four minutes early. Don't worry, he'll be here.'

'He better be. I'm not going back to that bloody prison!'

'Shhh! What if someone hears you?'

'I'm not going back. If I go back I'm telling them all about you!'

'He's. . . He's. . .' Come on, Norman. He wouldn't let her down like that, he *wouldn't*. He was just having trouble parking, or—

A pair of headlights flashed on the other side of the railings. 'There!' She grabbed Geddes by the elbow and hurried her down the wheelchair ramp and out onto the road. Helped her into the back of the Volvo estate. Val sat up front with Norman and little Donald.

Geddes kicked the back of Norman's seat. 'About bloody time you showed up! And what the *hell* do you call these clothes then?'

Norman stole a glance at Val. 'There's a suitcase in the back: lots of different things. I didn't know what you'd like so—'

'Not more of that frumpy shite!'

'They're perfectly good clothes.'

'Yeah, if you're bloody *sixty*.'

Val fastened her seatbelt, making sure it didn't squash little Donald inside her coat. Really he should be in a car seat, but that would give the game away. Besides, it would mean letting go of him, and Norman was a *very* careful driver. 'Can we just go, please?'

The last train to Aberdeen didn't leave until ten past eleven, so they sat in the North Station car park on Blackwall Hill, eating fish and chips.

Geddes kicked the back of Norman's chair again. 'What time is it?' The words mumbled through a mouth full of chips.

'Ten fifty.'

'For fuck's sake. Where's my ticket?'

Norman sighed and handed it over. 'I've booked you into a little B&B for tonight, and a taxi in the morning to take you to the ferry, so—'

'And my money?'

Another sigh, only this time it came with an envelope.

Geddes ripped it open and counted the contents. 'Where's the rest of it?'

Val twisted as far round in her seat as she could without disturbing little Donald. 'That's all of it. That's what we agreed.'

'Aye, but I've been thinking. Wee Rolf's my flesh and blood, isn't he? I *love* the little bastard. Don't think I can give him up for a measly three grand. You know what I mean? Could get more than that sticking him on bloody eBay.' She smiled. 'I want seven.'

Silence settled into the car.

Norman looked away. 'We haven't got that much.'

'Borrow it. I've been watching them adverts for three days now: "Want a low-cost personal loan?" Seven thousand or I take the kid with me to Aberdeen.'

'We. . . It'll take days to get one sorted—'

'That's OK, you can send the money on. I'll just keep the wee sod till you get it.' She stuffed the envelope and its three thousand pounds down the front of her 'frumpy' top.

'No!' Val flinched back, her hands covering little Donald's head. 'You can't take him back! I *need* him!'

'Come up with the other four grand and he's all yours.' She opened the back door. 'Now give me the kid.'

Val grabbed Norman's arm, tears making the car blur. 'You can't let her take him!'

'I. . .' Norman bit his lip. 'I've got my redundancy money at the house.'

'How much?'

He closed his eyes. 'Enough.'

Kathy closed the door again. 'OK, let's go get it.'

Norman drove them down Shalster Road, sticking to the speed limit, not doing anything to attract attention. Past Montgomery Park, across the River Wynd, up into Castleview, then out through the city limits into the darkness.

'Where the hell do you two live, in a bloody cave?'

Val shook her head. 'It's a small cottage, on the other side of the hill. You know, by Dundas Woods?'

'You bloody would. Teuchters.'

Ten minutes later, the Volvo's wheels bumped through potholes as Norman coaxed the car up a rutted track into the forest, headlights casting thick shadows that writhed and squirmed through the undergrowth. The jolts made little baby Donald gurn – working himself up to a fully formed howl.

'How can you live way out here? You never heard of

civilization? Jesus. . . If you want to bring my kid up out here it's going to cost you *eight*. Poor bastard. You know I—'

Norman stopped the car. 'We're here.'

Geddes looked around, pressing her face up against the glass. 'Where the hell's the house?'

'Over there.' He pointed at a dark shadow lurking between the trees, then flicked on the interior light. 'Val, you want to stay here while I get the money?'

And that was when Donald started to howl.

'He'll be needing his feed. . .' Val slipped the baby from the sling and held him out to Geddes.

'No chance. Told you: my nipples are—'

'Please!'

She groaned at the car roof. 'Eight grand. Give me the little sod.'

Val handed him over and Geddes hauled up her top, popped out a pale swollen breast, and jammed it in Donald's screaming mouth. Two gurgles, then silence, then the sound of sucking. She scowled at Norman. 'What's the matter, never seen a tit before? Go get my bloody money.'

Blushing, Norman apologized, then clambered out into the night.

It took nearly half an hour for little Donald to stop and by then Geddes was glowering. 'Missed my bloody train now. And where's your shitty husband with my cash?'

She thrust the baby back at Val, then tucked her breast back into the saggy bra. A knock on the window and Geddes flinched. 'Aaagh. . . Dirty bastard's been standing out there watching the whole time. Probably having a wank.' She gripped her breasts and jiggled them at him. 'Take a picture, *pervert*!'

The door popped open and Norman leaned in. 'This is yours. . .' He smashed his fist into her face. She almost managed to scream before he hit her again, then dragged her out of the car by the ankles.

A rectangle of light spilled from the car's back door, spotlighting Norman as he dumped Geddes on the ground then walked around to the boot of the car and came back with a tyre-iron.

Geddes tried to scramble away into the bushes, but he grabbed her, held her down, battered her with the tyre-iron. Her body twitched as he beat the life out of it, wet thuds and muffled cracks swallowed by the quiet woods.

Afterwards they sat in the car, Val and her brave Norman, holding hands and gazing down at their new son. He was perfect.

'See,' Val beamed, more content than she'd ever been in her whole life, 'I told you it would work.'

'Yes. Yes, you did.' Norman leaned over and kissed her, then turned the car around and drove them home.

7: Swans a-Swimming

The sky sparkles in the pink glow of dawn: quarter past nine on a cold December morning and the air is crisp. Normally they'd go to the boating lake in Montgomery Park, but today is special. Today they're going out on the river.

Shrieks and giggles echo out across the dark, sluggish water as the small flotilla of rowing boats pushes away from Dundas House. The girls are noisy and boisterous: all keyed up because they've won the regional finals. Next stop: Edinburgh and the Scottish under fifteens' swimming championship. This is their day and they're going to enjoy it.

'Please, sir.' It's Sarah Morrison: breaststroke; tall and gangly with long ginger hair and a complexion like bleached bones; just on the cusp of twelve and changing from a confident wee girl into a shy teenager. 'Are we going to be on The Bellows long?'

James Kirkhill looks over his shoulder at the snail-shaped island in the middle of the river. A pair of dilapidated buildings cling to the rocks and grass, brooding silently. Mourning their missing inmates. The faded blue-and-white sign still says MacAndrew's Sanatorium, but no-one's been treated here since the end of World War II. 'About four hours, plenty of time to do some sketching, take some photos. . .' He nudged the hamper sitting at his feet. 'Have a picnic. Why?'

'Oh.' She blushes, looks away. 'I just wondered is all.'

James throws her a wink, even though he's old enough to be her grandfather. 'Got to be back in time for a hot date, is that it? Who's the lucky boy?'

Sarah's blush goes nuclear and the other two girls in the boat laugh. She mumbles something, and puts her back into the rowing. Her oar slices through the water. Sitting next to her, Danielle takes this as a challenge and matches her stroke for stroke.

'Slow down, slow down. . .' James holds up his hands, grinning. 'We'll end up in Norway at this rate. Got to give the rest of the team a chance to catch up.'

Danielle. She's got gold medal written all over her. Popular, mature beyond her years, friendly, attractive, smart, outgoing, and one hell of a swimmer. Give her another four years and she'll be *unstoppable*. Everything is going to happen for Danielle. She's radiant.

Half an hour later they're tying up at the old jetty, clambering up the stone steps and running all over the island.

James takes a deep breath and makes a loudhailer out of his hands. 'Be *careful*, no swimming, make sure you've got someone with you at all times!' His words echo impotently between the buildings' empty husks. 'I mean it!'

James wraps the scarf tightly around his neck and sets

out for a brisk walk around the island. Trying to keep warm. Eventually he finds a spot in the lee of the staff wing, where the morning sun has melted the frost from the grass. Leaving it a rich and vibrant—

'And were you alone at this point?'

James Kirkhill looked up from the table, blinking – as if he was trying to remember where he was.

Interview room number six was in the old part of Force Headquarters: peeling paint, stained carpet tiles, a scratched table and four creaky plastic seats. A storage radiator clunked away to itself in the corner, the smell of burning dust mingling with the sour armpit stink coming from DI George 'Stinky' McClain. Not his fault. It was glandular. But James Arnold Kirkhill didn't seem to notice, just sat there staring at the tabletop.

He was an English teacher at Kingsmeath Secondary: mid-fifties, slightly overweight, trendy oval glasses, and purple bags under his eyes. Wild grey hair and nine-p.m. stubble.

At least he'd stopped crying. According to the DS who'd interviewed him after the accident, the man could barely speak for blubbering.

'Was I alone? I think so.' He wrapped his arms around himself. 'It was the only warm place on the island and I'm . . . well, I broke my ankle a couple of years back and it aches when it's cold. I was going to read my book.'

'But you didn't?'

A frown. 'What?'

'You said you were "*going* to read your book". That implies something else came up.'

60

'Oh. . . No, just a turn of phrase. I was reading a Ruth Rendell.' A fleeting smile. 'My guilty secret.'

'OK. So it's just you and Ruth Rendell. No one else was there. Then what happened?'

'I've already been over all of this.'

'I know, but it's better if I hear it first-hand. In your own words.' There was a long pause. George drummed his fingers on the tabletop. 'You want a cup of tea, or something? I can get DC Richardson here fetch it if you like?'

Kirkhill didn't say a word, just shook his head and gave a long, shuddering sigh.

The girls are having a great time. It took some organizing – not many people visit The Bellows these days – but James knew they'd love it.

That's the great thing about coaching the under fifteens' swimming club: the enthusiasm. Give them a few years and they'll turn sullen and cynical. But right now they're still young enough to enjoy themselves without feeling self-conscious.

Well, everyone except Sarah. She sits off on her own, staring out over the Kings River towards the castle. Pining.

Probably thinking about her boyfriend.

James calls them all together at half past twelve. It's time for the picnic.

They come from all over the island, running, laughing, their breath streaming out behind them.

Danielle takes the role of 'Mother', handing out the sandwiches and vegetarian whatnots while he cracks open a couple of thermos flasks, pouring cream-of-tomato soup into polystyrene cups. The steam fogs up his glasses.

After lunch, they pack everything back into the picnic hamper and get in the boats for the trip home.

Sarah's distracted, her rowing sloppy. She's been chewing at her fingernails, worrying them down to the quick.

Danielle tries to cheer her up, but it doesn't work. She rolls her eyes at James and pulls a face. Isn't Sarah *silly*. . .

And then there's a loud thump and the boat lurches sideways. Danielle is half out of her seat, hauling on the oar when it happens. One minute she's in the boat, the next she's in the dark, swirling water.

Oh dear Lord. . .

It's a moment before anyone can react. James scrambles to the side of the boat, reaching for her, but she's gone.

Three feet from the boat: a flash of blonde hair, a flailing arm, a shriek. He grabs Danielle's abandoned oar and tries to reach her with it.

Splashing.

Panic.

Sarah screams.

Danielle surfaces again, bright-red blood coursing down her face. She splutters, arms and legs thrashing in the cold water, as—

'Thought you said she was a strong swimmer.' George sat back in his creaky plastic seat, frowning.

'She. . . We'd only just eaten. It was bitterly cold. The shock must have been terrible. Unable to breathe. . .'

'Why wasn't she wearing a life jacket?'

'I. . .' He shook his head. Shivered. 'I don't know, I thought she was, but it's all so difficult. . .'

'So you tried to reach her with the oar?'

* * *

62

She's drifting further and further from the boat, churning the water around her, head slipping beneath the surface. All around him the girls are screaming as he fights with the river for Danielle's life.

Too far away.

He shoves Sarah to the floor of the boat, grabs both oars and rows for all he's worth; muscles groaning, wood creaking. Faster: row *faster*.

This is his only chance. 'Grab my hand!'

She reaches, but her fingers slip through his. Danielle goes under again. James plunges his arm into the icy water, gritting his teeth against the pain. Grabbing for her. . .

She's struggling . . . so *cold* . . . and then she's gone.

'Her. . .' Kirkhill swallowed, the tears starting again. 'We found her body caught up on Calderwell Bridge. She. . . She was. . . Oh God. . .' He buried his head in his hands and sobbed.

'I see.' George pulled a sheet of paper from the pathologist's preliminary report. 'We did a post mortem on Danielle's body: just routine, we do them following any fatal accident. You've been a naughty, naughty boy, haven't you, Mr Kirkhill?'

The teacher stared at him, mouth going up and down, but nothing came out. He cleared his throat. 'I. . . I don't know what you're talking about.'

'No? You mean you don't remember sexually assaulting a girl in your care?'

'What?' His eyes widened. 'No. . . I never!'

'Come off it, Kirkhill. The pathologist says Danielle was sexually active, and guess what happened when we went through her diary?' He held up a clear evidence pouch with a hard-backed jotter in it. The pink cover was festooned with blue biro hearts.

'I never touched her, I swear!'

'She was pretty – I saw her before they cut her open – very well-developed for a twelve-year-old. Did you tell her you'd make her a woman?'

'I never touched her!'

'How about this then?' George pulled the pink diary out of the evidence bag and flipped it open. A yellow post-it note marked the place. 'Thirteenth of July. "James came to me after swimming practice today. He looks so handsome in his new glasses. He waited till all the other girls were gone then kissed me in the showers. I was trembling and naked, but he—"'

'It never happened! She's making it up!'

'"—took me in his arms, the warmth of his body burning through his tweed jacket—"'

Kirkhill grabbed George's arm, pulling the book away. 'Look, it happens all the time. The girls: they get a crush on their teachers. It's a difficult age for them, all those hormones. It's just fantasy!'

'Fantasy?'

'Yes!'

'I see.' George nodded. 'So you won't mind giving us a DNA sample then?'

'DNA. . .?'

'If it's just a fantasy.'

'I. . .'

'To be honest, it doesn't really matter if you want to, or not. I'm detaining you on suspicion of sexually abusing a minor. That means I can get fingerprints, blood, urine, DNA, whatever I want.'

'But—'

'And then we'll see if your DNA is a paternal match for the foetus Professor Muir cut out of Danielle this afternoon.'

Kirkhill sat there with his mouth hanging open. Like a startled fish. 'I. . . But. . .'

George held the book up and started reading again, '"It hurt a little at first, but it was so beautiful having him deep inside me. Thrusting, thrusting. . ."'

It only took the Identification Bureau's forensic science lab an hour and a half to make the match. James Thomas Kirkhill was the father.

Kirkhill stared at the report on the table in front of him. 'Danielle was . . . she was more mature than anyone I'd ever met. Always knew what she wanted and how to get it. I mean she was *brilliant*, but manipulative with it. . .' He licked his lips. 'But I never did anything improper! Nothing. I loved her, yes, but it was . . . it was a *spiritual* love. I never laid a hand on her.'

'So how come she's carrying your kid then? Second Coming is it? Immaculate Conception?'

'I. . .' He picked at the skin around a fingernail until it bled. 'I was going through a bout of depression, the anniversary of Molly's death, I'd been drinking.'

'And you thought you'd just help yourself to some hot twelve-year-old-schoolgirl action?'

'No!' Kirkhill shook his head, tears sparkling in the overhead lights. 'Danielle turned up unannounced. I was about halfway through a bottle of Bowmore. Just going to drink the day away, get it over with. Try not to think about those last six months in the hospital, watching her die. . .' He sniffed, wiped his face with a wrinkled hand. 'Danielle said she wanted to make it all better, kept pouring whisky into me. I was drunk, I didn't know what I was doing! She set the whole thing up. . . The next day at school she's telling me we're meant to be together.' He blinked up at George, eyes glistening. 'She made the whole thing happen.'

George placed the DNA report back in the file. 'And did she make it happen again?'

Kirkhill's mouth fell open. 'No! Never! She wanted to, but I wouldn't let her!'

'So how come her diary's full of the pair of you shagging?'

He grabbed George's hands. 'Please, you've got to believe me: she's making it all up! She wasn't like other girls her age, she was . . . so *focussed* on what she wanted. It's why she was such a great swimmer, and—'

'Not that great a swimmer: she drowned.'

'I swear to you, I never laid a hand on her. Not since that first time when she got me drunk. Never.'

George took his hands back, tilted his head to one side, and gave Kirkhill a good hard stare.

Poor old git was probably telling the truth. There was something about girls that age that always made George's flesh crawl. Like you could hear the Machiavellian wheels spinning inside them. People thought young men were the aggressive ones, but young women were fucking vicious. And Kirkhill was obviously wracked with shame and guilt. A grown man outmanoeuvred by a twelve-year-old girl.

George was about to suspend the interview when DS Raith barged through the door and waved a manila folder at him. 'Sorry to interrupt, Guv, but you might want to take a look at these.' She stood against the wall, face impassive as George flicked through the report and attached pictures.

'You. . .' He cleared his throat and stared at Kirkhill. 'You say that it only happened the one time, and that Danielle was responsible?'

The teacher nodded.

'Well, want to have a go at explaining how these got onto your home computer then?' He slapped the pictures down on the tabletop, one after the other. A series of explicit, hard-core pornography, all featuring Danielle and her school swimming coach – James Kirkhill.

Then another set: a different girl this time, with ginger hair and a bone-pale complexion. And another one.

Kirkhill flinched. 'They. . . They're not mine. Someone else must have put them on my computer . . . to discredit me! It was—'

'You're in the bloody photos! And according to this you've got about two and a half gig of assorted kiddie porn on there too!'

Kirkhill stammered, fidgeted, eyes flicking from George to the door and back again. 'I never . . . it . . . no . . . you see—'

'You know what they do with paedophiles in Oldcastle nick? Sometimes they get stabbed, sometimes they get the shit kicked out of them, and there was this one bloke got raped with a broom handle. Died a week later: internal bleeding.'

It was like watching a building collapse, one minute James Kirkhill was there, the next there was nothing left but tears and snot and trembling, pale skin.

* * *

His hand swirls through the icy water, nothing, nothing, nothing . . . hair. He grabs at it, holding firm. Pull her to safety and everything will be all right. Everything will be—

She comes to him, in his little suntrap, smiling that smile she knows he loves. The one that makes his trousers bulge. Danielle grabs his hands and spins him around. Laughing. 'I've got some news for you. *Great* news.' She stops twirling and places one of his hands on her belly. 'Our love has caused a little miracle.'

No, no, no. . .

'You have to get rid of it! You're too young, your career. . .' Sweat sticks his shirt to his back. 'Think about the championships, the *team*!'

'James?' She backs off a couple of steps and stares at him, mouth a thin hard line. 'We are *keeping* this baby, and *you're* going to be the father, understand?' A smile lights her face like a burning building. 'We'll be the perfect family. And if not, I'll tell my mother. And she'll tell the police.'

—holding her head beneath the water as she struggles and struggles . . . and then she's gone, hanging lifeless beneath his fingers as that stupid bitch Sarah screams.

He lets Danielle go.

There will always be more where she came from.

8: Maids a-Milking

Filling telephone boxes with soft-core pornography wasn't a bad job in the height of summer, but on a freezing Tuesday night in December it was an absolute bastard. Brian reached into his armpit and dragged out the Blu-Tack – the only way to keep the damn stuff warm enough to stick – tore off a blob, pressed it onto the back of a postcard and fixed it above the phone. SEXY SADIE, THE NAUGHTY LADY with a photo of an attractive, big-boobed blonde in thigh-high leather boots, matching basque, and whip. Whoever the girl in the picture was, she was nothing like the old dear who actually answered the accompanying phone number. The *real* Sexy Sadie looked like Brian's nan.

The phone box was already pretty crowded. There was Mr Aziz's finest – Sexy Sadie, Busty Becky, and Naughty Nikki – and the usual collection of doms, subs, trannies, tarts and rent boys. Some had photos, others just the promise of personal visits and 'unique services'. Brian tore them all down, leaving the box clean except for Mr

Aziz's doddery bunch of kinky pensioners, and Dillon Black's girls.

Brian might be failing geography, but that didn't mean he was stupid.

Hands jammed deep into his pockets, he nipped across the road, taking his chances with the traffic. The burger joint was busy: hordes of kids eating processed meat and fries, passing around cans of super-strength lager when the staff weren't looking.

A couple of them nodded hello as he walked in.

Cameron Williams glanced up from his double cheeseburger, mouth hanging open – full of half-chewed mystery meat. 'Oy, Wanker!' Doing the hand gesture as well.

Brian ignored him. Cammy was a dick. But he was a *big* dick and answering back would just get Brian's head kicked in.

So he joined the queue for till number three instead.

He shuffled forwards, staring at the menu like he didn't already know it off by heart. Cheeseburger with onion rings, fries, and a large Irn-Bru – same as always. And, as it was bloody freezing outside, one of them deep-fried apple pie things as well.

Bob – his mum's new bloke – slipped him a tenner to get something to eat while they went down the pub. Which was cool. Meant he'd have enough left over for a packet of fags and a couple bottles of extra strong cider. That'd round off the evening nicely.

He ordered his burger, then settled back against the counter to wait. Checking his pockets: still twenty or thirty postcards to go. That would take him all the way down to the railway station, where there was a nice little corner shop that didn't mind selling booze and fags to thirteen-year-olds. The free-market economy in action: that's what his English teacher, Mr Kirkhill called stuff like this.

Brian knew *all* about the free-market economy. He was a seasoned practitioner of its darker arts.

The food arrived and he carried it over to an empty table; it was way too cold outside to eat in some piss-smelling shop doorway. He took a big bite of burger and a shadow fell across the table.

A man's voice, deep and gravelly: 'Anybody sittin' here, mate?'

Brian shrugged and kept on eating, head down. Free country, wasn't it?

The bloke plonked himself on the other side of the table and unwrapped whatever it was he'd ordered.

'You're Brian, right? Brian Calder?'

Brian shrugged again, still not looking up. 'Depends, doesn't it.'

'Thought I recognized you. We're in the same line of work, Brian.'

'Oh aye?' Why did the weirdoes always have to sit next to him?

He crammed in an onion ring, and took a peek at the nut-job: thin, pasty-faced, goatee beard, hooded eyes and wide forehead, hair like one of them teddy boys you saw on the Discovery Channel, and a diamond ear stud. Fingertip-length black leather jacket over broad shoulders, a Hawaiian shirt and shark's tooth necklace. Big Johnny Simpson.

Oh Jesus. . .

Brian's cheeseburger tried to choke him. He coughed, spluttered, forced it down. 'Mr Simpson.' He dragged on

71

a smile. 'Nice to see you.' Oh Christ. . . 'How's Leslie?'

'Fuck should I know? I'm only her father.' Big Johnny took a bite of his not-so-happy meal. 'Bloody kids: soon as they hit puberty they want nothin' to do with their old man.' Chew, chew chew.

'Right. Right.' Oh God. . .

Big Johnny polished off the burger, fries and a large Diet Coke, then settled back in his plastic seat and stared at him. 'You finished?'

Brian glanced down at his food – virtually untouched, the melted cheese all leathery-looking, the onion rings pale and greasy. 'Not really hungry.' Not any more.

'Good.' Big Johnny stood, towering over the table. Shite: he was *huge*. 'Come on, you and me are goin' to take a little walk.'

Brian's newly dropped balls tried to claw their way back into his body.

Oh fuck. . .

Half past eight and the city lights made sparkling reflections in the Kings River. Brian had a perfect view of them, because Big Johnny was dangling him – head down – over the water. A truck rumbled by on the bridge above, pigeons cooed on the metal support beams. Brian clenched his arsehole tight shut. Don't cry. Don't puke. Don't beg for Mummy. . . She'd be pissed by now anyway.

It was pitch-black under the Calderwell Bridge, just the red tip of Big Johnny's cigarette, bobbing up and down as he spoke. 'You see, Brian, people who screw with me end up in the water. If they're lucky.' He gave Brian's ankles a shake. 'You feeling lucky?'

'It wasn't me!'

'Eh?' Johnny puffed on his fag for a bit. '*What* wasn't you?'

'Leslie – I didn't do it!'

There was silence, then the shaking started again in earnest. 'What about Leslie? What the fuck *didn't* you do?'

'Get. . .' Change fell out of his pockets, splashing into the dark waters over his head. 'Get her up the stick!'

'SHE'S FUCKING PREGNANT?'

'It wasn't me!'

'She's fourteen!'

'Please, I didn't do it!' Brian closed his eyes – this was it, he was going to die.

'*Bastard*.' Big Johnny let go.

Brian fell, screamed. THUMP – flat on his back, the footpath slamming the air from his lungs. Mummy. . . He lay there, spread-eagled, gripping the cold, dirty concrete.

Johnny grabbed him by the scruff of the neck and yanked him upright. 'Who was it?'

'I don't know, it—'

Johnny backhanded him one.

'I don't know, I don't!' The words tasted of old pennies.

'Then you find out, understand? You find out who's been . . . *touching* my little girl and you tell me, or I swear to God: you're going for a fucking swim next time!'

Brian nodded, tears spilling down his face, top lip wet with snot.

Johnny took a couple of steps away, dragging on his cigarette like he was punishing it. 'You know what? I need a drink. You need a drink?' He flicked the dying gasp of his cigarette out into the cold, dark river. 'Course you do.'

* * *

73

The Docker's Arms was a shit-hole pub down by the Logansferry harbour: stained wallpaper, cracked and sticky linoleum, vinyl upholstery held together with silver tape. A CD player belted out hits by Jimmy Shand and His Band – accordion music to drink heavily by. The choice was Export or Lager. None of your fancy real ales, pilsners or alcopops here. Big Johnny got them each a pint of Export and a double whisky. The wrinkled old lady behind the bar didn't seem to care that Brian was only thirteen.

'Mairi's Wedding' crackled out of the speakers as Big Johnny led the way to a table in the corner. He sat and watched Brian gulp down the whisky. Pulled out a packet of fags and lit one – looked like the old lady didn't care about the smoking ban either. 'You did no' bad there. I've known grown men pee themselves when I dangle them.'

Brian managed a sickly smile and reached for his pint.

'I hear you've been selling some stuff.'

Deep drink. Gulp. Nod.

'Who're you selling for? Dillon?'

'Nah.' Brian shook his head, the whisky burned in his half-empty stomach. 'I . . . I get some blow off this bloke I know from Blackwall Hill, he gets it from someone in Dundee.'

'Not any more.' Big Johnny dug a rolled-up carrier bag out of his leather jacket and dumped it on the table. 'Now you work for me.'

Brian opened the bag and peered inside. A couple of ounces of blow and about two dozen silver paper wrappers. 'I . . . I've never sold—'

'Heroin's like anything else: you hand it over, they give

74

you the money. No problem. Like sellin' tins of beans, or washing-up liquid. Only the mark-up's way better.'

'But—'

'You're no' looking for another swimmin' lesson, are you, Brian?'

'No! No, it's fine, I can do it.'

Big Johnny smiled. 'Knew you'd see it my way.' He reached into his other pocket and pulled out a small leather bum-bag. 'You put the money in here. *All* of the money. You get your commission when I get the cash. If you *ever* help yourself we go back to the bridge, only this time I'm taking a claw hammer with me. Understand?'

Brian nodded.

'Good. Now finish your drink and get to work.'

The blow was easy enough to get rid of – half the kids in Brian's class liked a spliff – but the smack was a different matter. It was too hardcore for Brian's mates. Too *dangerous*. Which was why he was wandering round Kingsmeath's skanky red-light district in the middle of the bloody night. It wasn't a patch on the upmarket 'tolerance zone' over in Logansferry. Here the hoors were unregulated, unprotected, and probably infectious. Milking the punters for all they were worth.

But at least he wasn't going to get his balls cut off by some pimp. This lot were strictly freelance.

Brian hit pay dirt with the very first girl he tried: a stick-thin figure with hollow cheeks and dark eyes, wearing just enough clothes to stave off hypothermia. She took three wrappers.

Looked like Big Johnny was right – it was a piece of piss after all.

Brian made his way down the street, stopping to chat with the prozzies, blushing when they flirted with him, taking their money.

By quarter to twelve he was down to his last wrapper. Get a shift on and he could just make the Corner Emporium before it shut. Cider, fags and a packet of rolling papers – been skimming the blow all night, selling people quarter-ounces of hash that weren't *quite* up to size. Keeping enough for himself to get nice and high. Not stealing from Big Johnny Simpson, stealing from the customers. Not the same thing.

All he had to do was—

A woman in her early twenties with a mascara-streaked face and torn tights pawed at his sleeve. 'You got any more?' Her jacket was dirty up one side, hanging open to reveal a pale stomach, short skirt and low-cut top. She'd been pretty once, but it was a while ago. 'C'mon, I'm dying here. Maggie says you've got!'

Brian gave her a smile. 'It's your lucky day.' He held up the wrapper. 'Last one.'

She licked her lips, fingers stroking her dead-fish belly, eyes shining. 'How much?'

Brian told her and she swore.

'You're kidding – that's *twice* what Dillon charges! It's—'

'Take it or leave it.'

'But it's been a shite night. . . I'm good for it!' Wringing her hands, staring at the sparkling tinfoil. 'I'll pay you back.'

'Sorry, love, it's the rules. The guy I work for. . .'

She opened her coat wide and pulled up her top, showing off her naked breasts.

'He . . . er. . .' Brian blinked. Coughed.

'Come on, you know how it works.' She fumbled with his flies, groping her way into his underpants with cold fingers.

'It. . . But. . . Oh!' All available blood was diverted south.

She smiled at him, showing off a mouth full of fillings. 'Oh yeah, you like that, don't you?' Stroking. 'You give me the stuff and I'll see you right. Fine upstanding boy like you. I'll be gentle. . .' She sank down to her knees.

Brian grinned all the way home.

A dark-blue BMW was parked outside his house: alloy wheels, spoiler, tinted glass. Nice motor, even with the long scrape down the passenger side. The driver's door opened and Big Johnny stepped out. 'Well, if it isn't my little captain of industry.'

'Mr Simpson!' The smile died on Brian's lips.

'How'd you get on tonight?'

'Oh, you know. . .'

'Got my money?'

'I . . . erm. . .' He unbuckled the bum-bag and handed it over. 'All there, Mr Simpson. Like you said.'

'Uh-huh. . .' Big Johnny opened the zip and counted the money inside. 'You got any gear left?' He held out his hand.

Oh Christ: he knew about the missing wrapper.

Brian's mouth went dry. How? How did he know?

Don't just stand there, gob hanging open like a mong, tell him something. *Lie.*

The blow – give him the skimmed blow!

'I got some hash left!' Brian handed it over. 'Everything else is sold.'

'I see.' Johnny examined the small lump of dark brown resin. Probably weighing it up against the amount of cash in the bag. Trying to tell if Brian was screwing with him. Planning another trip to the Calderwell Bridge.

'I . . . I also found out who Leslie's been seeing.'

'Oh yeah?' The voice was low, dangerous. Like a Rottweiler. 'Who?'

'Erm. . .' BLAME SOMEONE: ANYONE! 'Cammy!' Yeah, Cammy would do – smart thinking. The guy was a total dick anyway, he *deserved* a visit from Big Johnny Simpson.

'Cammy?'

'Cameron Williams – he's a fourth-year at Kingsmeath Secondary.'

Johnny nodded. Stuck the lump of cannabis in the bum-bag. 'Get in the car.'

Back under the Calderwell Bridge: half past one in the morning.

Snow fell from the dark-orange sky, disappearing as it hit the swirling black water.

Don't. Look. Down.

Brian grabbed the rust-flecked support girder with cold trembling hands. The sound of muffled sobbing came from the lump on the footpath below – Cammy, hands tied behind his back, gag in his mouth, a bag over his head, jeans soaked through where he'd pissed himself.

Big Johnny glanced up at Brian. 'Loop the rope over the lumpy bit.'

Brian did what he was told, chucked the other end onto the concrete path, then shinned back to safety. Well . . . you know, not counting the homicidal madman.

By the time he'd got down, Big Johnny was hauling on the rope, dangling Cammy out over the water – within arm's reach.

They'd picked him up on Patterson Street – staggering home on his own, out of his face on supermarket vodka. It hadn't been hard to bundle him into the back of the car. Tie him up. Stuff an old rag in his mouth. Keep him from screaming.

Brian shifted from foot to foot, stomach lurching, heart thumping, blood fizzing in his ears.

It'd be OK. Nothing to worry about. Right?

Big Johnny was just going to scare Cammy: like he'd scared Brian. That was all this was, just a bit of terror to teach the bastard a lesson.

Even if it wasn't his lesson to learn.

'*Clunk*,' and Big Johnny was back at the car boot. He pulled out a plastic bag from that big DIY superstore on the south side of the city and tossed it over to Brian. There was a set of decorators' coveralls inside, the kind the police wore on the telly when they dug up some serial killer's basement.

Johnny dug out another pair of coveralls and clambered into them. 'Put it on.'

Was harder than it looked, but he managed. Then it was blue plastic bags over their shoes. And a pair of latex gloves.

That's when Big Johnny produced the knife.

Cammy just hung there and cried.

Johnny grabbed him and sliced through the fourteen-year-old's clothes, cutting them away – even the piss-soaked trousers and pants. He dumped the rags in a bin-bag, leaving Cammy stark-bollock naked, shivering, covered with goose pimples. Sobbing behind the gag.

Big Johnny made one last trip to the boot of his car and came back with a baseball bat. 'You know what a *piñata* is, you piece of shit? No?' Pause. 'How about you, Brian?'

Brian knew, but the words wouldn't come out – just this weird squeaking noise.

Big Johnny was scaring Cammy, that's all: just scaring him.

'No?' Johnny sighed. 'What the hell they teachin' you lot in school? A *piñata* is something you hit and hit and hit until the insides come out. Like this. . .'

It took fifteen minutes.

And Brian stood there, mouth open, trying not to be sick.

Say something: tell Johnny that it was all a lie. Cammy didn't touch his daughter. It was all just a wee white lie to stop him asking about the missing wrapper of heroin.

But he didn't say a word.

Because he had a pretty good idea what Big Johnny would do if he found out Brian had lied to him. And stolen from him.

And he'd rather feel guilty than dead.

9: Ladies Dancing

Andy 'Twitch' McKay sits at the bar with a pint of Export, a broken nose and the tail-end of a bad amphetamine buzz.

The Silver Lady is your swankier kind of titty bar – a long, low room with mirrors all along the back of the stage, so you can see the girls dancing from all angles. Leather seats, dark carpet, mirror ball sending bright chips of light sweeping across the small crowd. Not Twitch's kind of place at all. Nah, he's more of a 'Monk and Casket' kind of guy. Somewhere intimate, where he can get a beer with his mates, and maybe smoke a joint in the toilets. Where everybody knows his name.

Which is why he's steering clear of the place. Keeping under the radar. Playing it *coooool*. And watching Kayleigh Jacobs work.

Hard dance music pulses from the speakers, trying to make a quiet Wednesday sound like a busy Saturday, giving Kayleigh something to dance to. She's gorgeous: long legs, tight stomach, firm breasts, all done up in lacy underwear, sliding up and down her shiny pole like she's shagging the arse off it.

Oh yeah. . . Twitch could be that pole. If he had the cash for a lap dance. And maybe a bottle of vodka. And a few lines of something choice. Something to take the edge off.

But he's skint. The thieving bastards running the place cleaned him out with the cover charge and one drink. Now all he's got is the fluff in his pockets, the shivering cold sweats, and the laptop sitting at his feet – the only thing left from a wee spot of breaking and entering last week. Easily flog a wee computermabob like that, though. *Especially* somewhere like this. Might even get a couple hundred quid for it. Enough to keep him in booze and drugs for a couple of days. With a bit left over so Kayleigh can make him feel special.

The number finishes and Twitch launches into thunderous applause, wolf whistling as Kayleigh takes her bow. She turns and struts offstage into the wings. A brunette comes on next, the music swells, the new girl bumps and grinds, and Twitch goes back to his pint. Watching the door in the mirror behind the bar.

His reflection's looking better: the black eyes have faded. And yeah, his nose looks like a wonky doorknob, and makes this squeaky whistling noise when he breathes. Prominent cheekbones, sunken eyes, stubble. Hair long at the back and short on top: it's a 1980s classic. Fuck anyone who says different. Camouflage hoodie top and drainpipe trousers. Strung out, fucked up, and no good.

Christ knows why they let him into the Silver Lady. Must be desperate to make the numbers up tonight.

He takes a sip of beer and scans the punters in the mirror. Not many people in yet: a half-dozen guys out on a stag night; a pair of suits, drinking champagne and whooping at the girl on stage; and a couple of sad pervs, sitting on their own.

None of them want to buy a laptop.

There's a flurry of activity just after nine – a dozen pissheads, all done up in Santa hats. They order whisky and vodka, then hoot and cheer as Kayleigh comes back on for her third set of the evening. Animals. How can't they see she's only got eyes for Twitch?

She's spectacular. Lithe – almost rubbery – making him moan.

After she's done – sashaying off the stage to a standing ovation, her pert buttocks oiled up and glistening – he tries the laptop on the drunken Santa hats, but they ignore him, not taking him on, not wanting anything to do with a scheemie wee junkie like him. Scared in case they catch something. He leaves them alone before somebody calls security.

No one's ever going to buy this bloody computer. Might as well give up. Finish his shitey pint and go home.

Twitch slouches back to the bar and stares at the last inch of beer in his glass.

Maybe it's time to get out of town? Give Oldcastle the heave ho and bugger off somewhere warmer and safer. Like Dundee, or Perth, or Hell. Even *Aberdeen* would be better than hanging about here, waiting for Dillon to find him.

Yeah, it was definitely time to get—

A hand on his shoulder. Twitch flinches, squeals, wraps his arms around his head. 'Jesus, you're jumpy!' West coast accent, soft and lyrical: female.

He peers out between his fingers as Kayleigh slips onto the stool next to his. She's changed into a pair of leather trousers, high-heeled boots, a white crop top and a frock coat in red satin. Up close, she's even more of a stunner. Like one of them Greek goddesses.

She waves to the barman. 'Steve, give us a V-and-T, and another pint for Mr Jumpy here. Least I can do for scaring the shite out of him.' She smiles and he melts, except for one part which gets very, very hard.

'Wow . . . thanks.' This time the Export tastes of angels in baby oil.

Kayleigh takes a sip of her drink and leans on the bar.

Twitch coughs, crosses his legs to hide the stiffie. 'Er. . . Hi.' He sticks his hand out. It looks reasonably clean. 'The name's Twitch,'

'Yeah?' she looks at him over the top of her glass, but doesn't take his hand. 'That fits. I'm Kay—'

'Kayleigh Jacobs. I know. I'm. . .' Don't sound like a dick, don't sound like a dick. 'I'm a great fan of your work.'

She laughs, tossing her head back. Her long blonde hair swishes up and over her shoulder. 'Well, aren't you a smooth bastard?'

He grins. 'Thanks.' This is exactly how it's meant to happen, Twitch McKay: suave, sophisticated, and funny. She'll see there's more to him than the tatty clothes and the skittering drugs. He's a *man*.

Kayleigh disappears off to the toilets, and when she comes back she runs a perfect fingernail down his arm. 'You fancy a private dance?'

Shite. . . 'Sorry, I kinda came out without my wallet.'

She smiles. 'It's OK. I like you. It'll be my little treat.'

She bites her bottom lip and takes his hand, leading him away from the bar and through a little door on the far side of the club.

The private dance room's not much bigger than Twitch's bedroom at home: six foot by eight foot, with a large vinyl sofa and a small coffee table. She points at the sofa. 'Sit down and keep your hands to yourself. That's very, *very* important.' Kayliegh slips off her blood-red coat. 'You can look, and *I* can touch, but you can't. If you do, some- one will come in and hurt you. Do you understand?'

Twitch nods.

Play it cool.

Oh shit this is GREAT!

'Good.' She opens a wee unit and flicks a switch. Music fills the room as Kayleigh goes into her routine. Stripping for him, peeling off her high-heeled boots, trousers, top, till there's nothing left but red lace.

Her skin's perfect, her body's perfect, *she's* perfect. Oh God. . .

Just one touch. She'd understand, right?

She *likes* him.

There's a sound down the alleyway, like someone being sick, and then they're gone. Leaving Twitch alone in the darkness with his pain. He tries to clamber to his feet, but something explodes inside his head and he slumps back against the wall.

The man howches, then spits in Twitch's face. His voice is like a shallow grave. 'You want to try that again?'

'I'm sorry. . .' He stays where he is and gets a kick in the ribs as a reward.

'You're sorry?' Pause. 'Oh, that's all right then, isn't it?

You're sorry and everything's forgiven, aye?' The man squats down in front of him, grabs his hair and hauls his head up. Bangs it off the brick wall.

'Dillon, I—'

'No, you don't dare "Dillon" me, Andy McKay. We ceased to be on first fucking name terms when you screwed up that B-and-E. You call me *Mister* Black.'

'Mister Black, I—'

Dillon backhands him, the leather glove breaking Twitch's nose again. Fresh blood steams in the cold alley. 'Did I give you permission to speak?'

Twitch just whimpers.

'Right, here's how this works: I promised to write off your debt if you stole that painting for me. Nice and easy. Only you didn't, did you? You didn't get my painting, you fucked up!' A hard right hook snaps Twitch's head back into the wall again, making the world scream. 'No painting means you have to give me back the thirteen thousand you owe me, plus another week's interest. Let's call it fourteen thousand all in. Where is it?'

Twitch whimpers again.

'You can answer that one, Stupid.'

'I . . . I don't. . .'

'Ooh, bad luck.' Dillon grabs Twitch's arm, pulling it straight out then twisting it over, so it's elbow up. Then he drops all his weight on the joint. CRACK!

There's a small pause, then the pain hits – like a million rusty needles ripping through his veins.

Twitch opens his mouth to scream, but Dillon smashes a fist into it, cutting him off.

Dillon lets go and the arm flops to the tarmac. Eyes watering, nose streaming with blood, Twitch picks it up with his right hand and cradles it against his chest. Crying like a baby.

Dillon grins at him. 'Don't know what you're blubbing for: you've still got two legs to go, haven't you?'

'Please!' Oh fucking *Christ* it hurts!

'Please what?'

'Please, Mister Black. . .' He stares up at the man towering over him. 'Please, God, no. . .'

'Rules are rules, Twitch. If I let you away with it, every bugger will think I'm going soft. Next thing you know I'm getting no respect. Can't have that, can we?'

'Please!'

Dillon picks up one of the beer crates stacked at the back door of the club, whistling while he works. He clunks it down on the concrete and props Twitch's feet up on it, straight out in front of him.

'Oh, God, please don't. . . Please! I've got a computer, a laptop, you can have it! I stole it from that guy's house. It's yours!'

Dillon looks down at him. 'OK. Thanks, I appreciate the gesture.' Then he grabs a length of steel pipe and smashes it into Twitch's legs, hammering again and again. Pulverising the bone. The screaming only lasts for a few minutes, then everything . . . goes . . . black.

Kayleigh stands in the shadows, leaning heavily against the wall, as Dillon turns the skanky wee bastard's legs into mush. The left side of her face is tender and swollen, her ribs ache: and so do her breasts and legs. But that's nothing compared to how it stings and burns inside.

Dillon finally steps away from the mess. Panting.

She sniffs. 'Is he dead?'

'Nope.' Dillon smiles at her. 'This wee shite's going to spread the word about what happens if you fuck with me.'

She limps forward and kicks the motionless body in the head.

Dillon laughs. 'You want him dead?'

'Fucker raped me!' She kicks him again. Then stomps on his chest. 'Going on and on about how much he loves me and how great it is I'm dancing only for him . . . and all the time. . .' Another kick.

Dillon picks up the laptop bag and slings it over his shoulder. 'You sure you want him dead?'

'HE FUCKING RAPED ME!'

'Fair enough.' Dillon hands her the metal pipe. 'You did me a favour: I'll do you one. He's all yours.'

She stops, dead. 'What?'

'Cave his head in.'

'I. . .'

'Go on – no one will ever know it was you.'

She drops the metal pipe. It clangs on the alley floor. 'I . . . I can't.'

'No?' Dillon looks at her, head on one side, like a cat. 'You sure?'

Her voice is barely a whisper, trembling as the tears start. 'He raped me. You said to keep him busy and he raped me.'

'I meant buy him a *drink*, you silly cow. Did I say anything about getting him all sexed up?'

She turns away, staring at the ground. 'No, Mr Black.'

Dillon sighs. 'Oh, for goodness' sake. . .' He grabs one of the black plastic bin-bags and empties it on the alley floor. Tins and bottles clatter on the concrete. 'Tell you what: I'll make it easy for you.' He takes a handful of Twitch's mullet and drags him backwards – until he's sitting slumped against the wall – then sticks the bag over his head.

Kayleigh stares at him, mouth open as Dillon wraps the ends of the bag around Twitch's throat and ties them in a tight little knot, just under the chin. The bag puffs up slightly as the raping bastard breathes out. Then constricts as he tries to breathe in.

Dillon takes off his gloves and sticks them in his pocket. 'If you want the wee shite dead: just leave him. You want him to live: pop a hole in the bag before he suffocates. Your choice. I'm off for a beer.'

He disappears back into the club.

The sound of singing filters in from the street, then a bus rumbling past, then someone shouts the odds at their boyfriend. Then a taxi. . .

Kayleigh watches as the bag inflates and deflates over Andy 'Twitch' McKay's head.

Out. . . In. . . Out. . . In. . .

His right hand trembles.

Out. . . In. . . In. . . In. . .

She bites her bottom lip and tries not to cry.

In. . . In. . . In. . . In. . .

A siren, high and thin, flashing past on the main road.

Out. . .

Still.

Kayleigh starts to sob.

10: Lords a-Leaping

There was something calming about the view from the castle's ruined battlements at night: down the steep, dark hill to Kings Park; across the swollen black river to Castle View and the Wynd. Streetlights made sparkling ribbons in the darkness, like a spider's web flecked with dew.

He raised the bottle to his lips as the first flakes of snow began to fall, drifting down through the cold night air. An 1896 Chateau Laubade Armagnac – over a thousand pounds a bottle – and he was swigging it like a wino. It smoothed its way into his chest with gentle, warming fingers. Keeping him safe against the chill. Blocking the pain from his broken finger.

Making him brave enough to do what had to be done.

Another swig then he gazes into the blackness before him. The cliffs are steepest here: the perfect spot for jumping. Just as soon as he's finished his Armagnac – it would be a shame to let something so perfect go to waste. When he's finished – *then* he'll go. . .

* * *

'. . . but most of all I'd like to thank our *honoured* guest for taking time out of his busy schedule to come open our new offices today.' The fat man steps back and leads the applause.

It's a featureless industrial unit, identical to all the other featureless industrial units in the Shortstaine business park. If it weren't for the blue plastic sign above the door – SCOTIABRAND TASTY CHICKENS LTD. THEY'RE FAN-CHICKEN-TASTIC! – you wouldn't even notice it. But tomorrow there'll be a big feature in the local rag – banging on about *'job creation'* and *'local economic growth'* – featuring everyone's favourite white-haired, avuncular MSP: Lord Peter Forsyth-Leven.

Peter smiles and holds his hand up, waiting for the noise to die down before launching into his 'it's a great pleasure/challenges of tomorrow/forward Scotland' speech. The same one he trots out for all these drab little official functions. Opening offices, dedicating park benches, planting trees, you name it – he gets dragged into it. But that's what happens when you're an MSP and a bona fide lord to boot. Sixty years of *noblesse oblige*.

He finishes with a joke about two old ladies from Castle Hill and Santa's magic sack, then unveils the tiny blue plaque commemorating this proud moment for Scotia-Brand Tasty Chickens Ltd.

Photographers flash, hands are shaken, everyone smiles, and *finally* he can escape.

He turns his back on the dismal little place and marches off towards his Bentley, plipping open the locks before he gets there. Other people in his position need a driver and a horde of staff before they'll go anywhere near the opening of a chicken slaughterhouse, but not him. He has 'the common touch', it says so in all the papers.

There's a man waiting for him, leaning against the fence by the car, hands in his pockets, smiling.

Peter's mother always maintained that you could learn everything you needed to know about a man by looking at his shoes. This one has black leather brogues, a long black overcoat, well-cut black suit, white shirt and a scarlet tie. Businessman. Probably with an invitation to another bloody opening.

'Mr Forsyth-Leven?' The man smiles and sticks out his hand.

Mister? Bloody cheek – he's a *lord*.

Peter works up a smile of his own. 'Can I help you?' He opens the car door – just to make sure the man knows he has places to go, people to see, decisions to make.

'More like the other way around: I want to talk to you about a unique investment opportunity.'

Here we go again.

'Well, that's very kind of you Mr. . . ?' No name is forthcoming. Some people have no manners. 'But I'm afraid you'd have to speak to my office about that. I think—'

'No.' The man holds up a hand. 'I think you'll want to deal with this personally. You see, the opportunity is specific to you and you alone.'

Of course it is. When is it ever not? Peter sighs. 'What is it?'

'Keeping you out of jail, you dirty child-molesting old fucker.'

A siren wailed somewhere in the night. The snow had slowly thickened – going from drifting icing sugar to dense fat flakes that fell steadily from the dark-orange sky. They stuck to his clothes and hair, made tiny proto-drifts in the clefts of the brick that would grow and grow through the night. Falling on his twisted, broken body at the foot of the cliff. Burying it from sight. Locking him away in its icy embrace.

He smiled and took another mouthful of Armagnac.

Getting near the bottom of the bottle now.

If the weather didn't change, it might be weeks before he was found. Maybe not until the spring. Months. And he'd make the headlines all over again. LORD PAEDO FORSYTH-LEVEN – BODY FOUND! His face was numb with cold and alcohol, but the tears still burned.

They sit in the Bentley, the man in the overcoat gazing out of the window, while Peter cries – one hand cradled against his chest, the other covering his face. Sobbing like a little girl. Which is ironically appropriate.

Finally, he sniffs and snivels to a halt, wipes his eyes and nose on a handkerchief.

The Man doesn't even look at him. 'You finished? Or do I have to break another finger?'

'I don't mean to do it. . . I just. . . Sometimes. . . I can't help it, they're—'

A hard slap shuts him up.

'I don't want to hear you *justify* why you fuck children, understand? Try telling me again and I'll beat the living shite out of you.'

'I'm sorry. . .' The tears are back.

'I'll bet you are: sorry you got caught. Shouldn't have left all that kiddie porn on your laptop where someone could just break in and steal it, should you?'

'I. . .' Peter hangs his head. All these years; someone was bound to find out eventually. But it doesn't make it any less painful. 'What. . . What do you want?'

'I want the painting. *The Pear Tree*. That'll do to start with.'

'The . . . *The Pear Tree*? But that's a Monet, it's worth. . .'

The Man stares at him, face impassive, like a slab of white marble.

Peter clears his throat. Brings his chin up. Shows some of the steel that makes him such a force to be reckoned with on the floor of the Scottish Parliament. 'And if I don't?'

'Two choices. One: I beat the shite out of you, then hand you – and your laptop full of kiddy filth – over to the police.'

For the first time in fifty-four years, Peter almost wets himself. He takes a deep breath. 'And two?'

'I take you out to Dundas Woods, break every bone in your body, then bury you alive.'

'I . . . I'll. . . You *wouldn't*—'

'Want to try for another fucking finger?'

'The painting! I'll give you the painting!'

The Man smiles. 'See, that's why you make such a good politician: you know when to compromise. Start the car – we'll go get it now.'

'But—'

'Now.'

Peter starts the car.

The electrician still hasn't finished installing the new burglar alarm when they get back to the house. Locking the stable door. . . Not that it really matters. In fifteen minutes the only thing worth protecting will be gone.

Peter parks the Bentley and clambers out. It's getting colder. He watches The Man slowly turn in a circle, taking in the house and its surroundings. Probably 'casing the joint', like they did on the television.

Fletcher Road is festooned with big Victorian homes, mansions, tall wrought-iron gates, walled gardens, and old money. This is where the city's elite live – the people who've kept the city running for generations. People like Peter.

The Man nods. 'Very impressive.' He frowns at the electrician screwing a blue and yellow plastic box to the outside wall. 'Shame it's one of the old two-five-fifties. Take a professional about forty seconds to short out the box and get in.' He smiles. 'If you like, I can recommend something a bit less . . . amateurish?'

Heat courses across Peter's cheeks. 'Can we just get on with this please?'

A shrug. 'Well, don't blame me next time some junkie scumbag robs you blind, OK?'

Peter turns his back on him and storms inside. The painting is in the dining room: a pear tree at sunset, one golden fruit hanging between the dark-green leaves, the sky a wash of raging fire, fading to indigo and black. It's the most expensive thing he's ever owned. It's worth more than the house. He trembles as he touches the frame.

There's a whistle behind him. Then, 'Beautiful. . .'

'My grandfather brought it back from France at the end of World War One. He. . .' He's about to launch into the story of how the old man bought it from Monet himself, when he realizes there's no point. The Man isn't

95

interested in art, he's only interested in what it's worth. 'It doesn't matter.'

Peter lifts the picture down from the wall and lays it on the table.

The Man unfurls a large holdall, then stands there, staring at the painting. 'First time I saw it: I was seven. My dad took me to this exhibition at the gallery. I remember looking at it and thinking, that's the most beautiful thing I've ever seen.'

Peter closes his eyes. Over the last forty years he's lent the painting only four times. He should have never let it out of the house. If he'd kept it *safe*, this man wouldn't be here now.

There's a zipping sound, and when Peter opens his eyes again *The Pear Tree* is gone.

The Man takes the holdall off the table and puts the strap across his shoulders. 'Get your lawyer to draw up the transfer of ownership. I want it sorted by the end of the week.'

End of the week: tomorrow – Friday the 23rd. 'That might not be possible. . .' his voice sounds flat and dead. He's lost everything. The painting's just the tip of the iceberg: after this it'll be money, jewellery, the car. *Everything* will be sold off. Stripped away until there's nothing left. And then The Man will either kill him, or hand him over to the police.

'Well, you'd better hope—' He's interrupted by Peter's mobile phone ringing – Wagner's *Tristan and Isolde*. Peter pulls the mobile out and answers it. Force of habit.

'Hello?'

'Pete? Pete, it's me: Tony.'

Peter groans. As if today wasn't bad enough.

'Pete, we've got big trouble!'

'It's too late.'

'*Too late? Shit! They're not there are they? Pete, are the police there? Oh FUCK!*'

Peter sighs. Tony has always been excitable – an unfortunate consequence of dealing in illegal images and video files.

'No, the police aren't here. I'm. . .' He looks at The Man who shakes his head. The meaning is clear: this is just between the two of them. 'Margaret's not doing too well.' Which was true enough. If he was lucky, the throat cancer would take her before the money ran out and The Man turned on him. She'd never have to know.

'*What the fuck do I care about your bloody wife? They've arrested someone: that fucking idiot school teacher. He'll talk!*'

Peter actually laughs. Throws his head back and laughs.

'*Pete? What the fuck's wrong with you? Did you not hear what I said? He'll turn us in!*'

The Man puts a hand on Peter's shoulder. 'What's so damn funny?'

'I want my painting back.' He grins like a maniac. 'They've arrested someone in the same . . . "club". And as soon as he talks it's all out in the open. You've just lost your leverage.'

'Like hell I have.'

'Everyone will know. I'll be ruined anyway. So tell whoever you like: it's not going to make any difference.' He pulls back his shoulders. 'Now give me back my bloody painting!'

There's a pause, then The Man narrows his eyes. 'Who is it? Who've they arrested?'

'James Kirkhill – he teaches English at Kingsmeath Secondary.'

'And they've not picked up anyone else in your "club"?'

'No.'

'Good.' The Man pats him on the back. 'Then I have another "investment opportunity" for you and your friends. . .'

The Armagnac was nearly finished, just one or two mouthfuls left and it would be time. One small step for mankind, one giant leap for Lord Peter Forsyth-Leven. It wasn't just his face that was numb now – his hands were like frozen claws, he couldn't feel his feet – but that didn't matter. Soon he wouldn't be feeling anything ever again.

All of the great things he'd done in his life – the charity work, the glittering political career – and this was going to be what he was remembered for.

Paedophile. Suicide. Murderer.

The first two he could have lived with, no pun intended, but not the last. That was too much to bear on top of everything else.

He drained the bottle, squinted at the empty glass, then threw it out into the void. For a moment it sparkled through the falling snow, turning end over end, fading from sight. He held his breath, straining to hear it smashing against the rocks below . . . but there was nothing. Just the wind and the snow and the night.

Peter clambered all the way up to the top of the battlement wall.

It was time.

The plan is simple: everyone in the 'club' chips in five thousand pounds, and that buys them a life. One human

98

life for thirty-five thousand pounds. Not that much really, when you think about it. Five thousand pounds to carry on like nothing had ever happened. Safe to continue with their private little . . . 'indiscretions'.

Five thousand pounds to have someone killed.

The Man wouldn't go until Peter gave him everyone's name, to make sure no one 'forgot' to pay, taking *The Pear Tree* with him. Leaving a shadow behind on the faded wallpaper. So Peter fills in the time pacing back and forth in the lounge. Drinking cups of tea. Marching up and down the stairs to check on Margaret. Sitting at the dining-room table, staring at the hole Monet's painting has left behind.

The call comes at half past nine – it's Tony, sounding like Christmas has arrived three days early. *'Did you see the news? They released the bastard on bail this afternoon. Found his body at eight – hanged in his bedroom. Suicide note, the whole works! He topped himself, we don't have to give your man a bloody penny. It's perfect!'*

Perfect.

Peter sits at the table and looks up at the shadow on the wall. 'What makes you think The Man didn't kill him and make it *look* like suicide?'

'Don't be. . .' A lengthy pause. *'Can he do that?'*

Peter almost laughs. 'Of course he can, but it doesn't matter, does it? He has our names. What do you think he'll do if we don't pay up?'

Another pause, and then a lot of swearing. *'You bastard! You put him onto us! You stupid, fucking, ignorant bas—'*

Peter hangs up, buries his head in his hands, and cries.

He's betrayed everyone: his family, his friends, his constituents, his city, even his fellow paedophiles. . .

There's only one more thing he has to do, and then it can all go away. There's no other choice.

Eighty feet, straight down.

He was too drunk to remember enough secondary school physics to work out how long it would take to hit the ground, or how fast he'd be going when he did.

Paedophile, suicide, murderer. . .

Could he let Margaret find out about the horrible things he'd done? That he'd arranged to have a man *killed*. No matter what that idiot Tony said, it was obvious The Man had staged James Kirkhill's suicide. The schoolteacher had died, just so Peter's secret would be safe. It was all his fault.

So he'd gone upstairs to Margaret's bedroom, kissed her gently on the forehead, lied to her about how beautiful she looked, then held a pillow over her face until she stopped struggling. She would never know what a monster she'd married.

Peter took off his glasses, closed his eyes and stepped quietly off of the battlements.

11: Pipers Piping

Dirty. Fucking. *Bastard*. Craig sat in the car, scowling out of the windscreen, grinding his teeth. Drinking steadily from a bottle of Highland Park. The whisky burned deep inside, stoking the fires.

The song on the radio dribbled to a halt. "Ha, ha! You're listening to Sensational Steve's Festive Funathon; hope you've all been good for Santa!"

Prick.

Then wailing and screeching erupted from the car's speakers – the Oldcastle Military Pipe Band murdering 'Silent Night'.

Craig turned his scowl from the windscreen to the car radio. Then smashed his fist into it. His knuckles creaked and stung: the skin tore across them, oozing blood. He screamed and swore, yanked his seat back as far as it would go and stomped his heel down on the plastic casing. Again and again and again. The music stopped.

One more swig of Highland Park then Craig rammed the cork back in, stuffed the bottle in a pocket of his long

Barbour coat, and dragged himself out of the car. He'd made an absolute cock-up of parking the thing, leaving it diagonally across two spaces, but it didn't matter.

He popped the boot and pulled out the shotgun.

Nothing mattered after today.

He didn't even pay and display.

'Ho, Ho, Ho. . .' Santa beamed, leaning down so he was eye-to-eye with the little girl. Cute wee thing: red hair and freckles, sucking her thumb, and peering round her mummy's leg. Bet she'd heard stories about Father Christmas all her life, but this was probably the first time she'd ever seen him in the flesh.

'What's your name, little girl?' Making the words all big and cuddly – not too loud, or the little buggers had a habit of peeing themselves.

She took her thumb out of her mouth. 'Thara.' Then plugged up again.

Santa, AKA Stephen Wilson, beamed at her.

It wasn't that bad a job: once you got past the crappy grotto made of chipboard; the bum-numbing throne; the padded suit that made sweat trickle down the crack of your arse; the beard that itched like a bastard; the never-ending loop of drive-you-psycho Christmas carols; and the snotty-nosed little sods demanding presents. *Other* than that, six weeks as a department-store Santa wasn't too demanding.

You say 'Ho, Ho, Ho'; you smile and wink; you don't sit them on your knee – in case someone thinks you're a paedo; and you don't ask for their mum's phone number, even if she's a total MILF. Because she's not going to give it to a fat guy with a beard anyway.

'And have you been a good little girl, Sarah?' Bit of chat: say your prayers, brush your teeth, work hard in school, and please accept this crappy plastic toy wrapped up in snowman Christmas paper.

The ginger kid's mum was *definitely* a MILF. 'What do we say to Santa, Sarah?'

'Thank you, Thanta.'

'Good girl.' She took her daughter's hand, and led her out of the grotto.

Thanta stared at Mummy's arse – it was like God had squeezed two perfect grapefruit into a sock. Sigh. . .

And: NEXT!

It was a lot more difficult to hide a shotgun under a long coat than it looked in the movies. The damn thing was nearly impossible to hold like that, especially with his hand all swollen and bleeding – he'd dropped it half a dozen times between the car and the lifts before figuring out a way to make it work. Craig took his left arm out of the sleeve and held the gun upside-down beneath the coat. Should have sawn the barrel off with a hacksaw. And all that whisky wasn't helping either; the world wouldn't stay in focus. How he'd got here without crashing the car into something was anyone's guess.

Craig screwed one eye shut and pressed the button for the lifts. Staggered a couple of steps backwards and one to the side as a woman wheeled a massive pushchair over from the MOTHER AND BABY parking spaces.

She stared at him – standing there swaying slightly, one arm hidden under his long wax coat. Probably thought he was some sort of drunken pervert. *Is that a shotgun in your pocket, or are you just pleased to see me?*

She glanced from the stairs, to the lifts, to Craig, and back to the stairs again. Then the lift went *ping* and the doors slid open. She shrugged and followed him into the brightly lit metal box.

'I'm. . .' Craig cleared his throat as the doors closed. The trick was to get all the words in the right order. Can't sound pished if all the words are in the right order. 'I'm not a perv . . . pervert.'

She didn't make eye contact, just stood there watching the floor numbers count down to ground level and escape.

'I'm hap . . . happily married.' He frowned. 'No, no, no: not happily. I was happily, but now I'm not. . . You know?' Silence. 'You . . . you see I *was* happy, but, but. . . She's sleeping with some . . . someone else!'

He paused to see if the woman would jump in with an expression of sympathy, but she kept her eyes on the numbers.

'You're right.' He leaned his head against the cool metal wall. 'I should shut up and leave . . . leave you alone.' He closed his eyes and waited for the elevator to shudder to a halt.

Ping. A sudden swelling of noise as the doors opened on the main shopping level. The squeak of buggy wheels. And then he was alone.

Craig took a deep breath and lurched out into the crowds, gripping the shotgun tight beneath his coat. It was time to go see Father Fucking Christmas.

Stephen wriggled in the throne. Had to be a position on this bloody thing that didn't make his arse eat itself. Be lucky if he didn't have piles by Boxing Day.

He gave his head elf the signal to send in the next one.

A wee boy with a runny nose. Then it was a wee girl called Ashley whose mother looked like a man in drag. And then another little boy called Simon, who wanted a dinosaur and a aeroplane and a puppy and a Action Man kung fu killer and a hat and a dinosaur and a chocolate house and, and, and. . .

Finally it was half-eleven: time for the statutory fifteen-minute pee-and-tea break. The head elf – a part-time goth called Greg, dressed up in a green tunic, green pointy hat, green curly-toed slippers and red-and-white striped tights – plonked the SANTA WILL BE BACK SOON! sign in front of the grotto's entrance. Then they both buggered off out the back.

The store had been kind enough to build the grotto over one of the service entrances, so Santa could go take a piss without the kiddies seeing him. And then, when the call of nature had been answered, Stephen doffed his fur-trimmed red hat, white wig and beard, and joined Greg the Christmas Goth in the stairwell for a sly joint, out of view of the security cameras.

Greg leaned back against the wall. 'So . . . doing anything exciting tonight?'

Stephen took another hit, holding the smoke in his lungs for as long as possible. Then wheezed it out. 'I wish. Taking my kid to go see that new animated thing: *Skeleton Bob and the Witch's Christmas*. She's mad on the books.'

'Any good?'

'Fucking doubt it.'

'Grievous.' Greg took another long drag.

'You got any gear for me?'

'Gear?' Greg gave a wee smoky laugh. 'Jesus, are you out of touch. Yes, granddad, I got some "gear". It's "groovy, man".' He even made little sarcastic quote bunnies with his fingers.

'Aye, very funny.' Stephen took one last hit then pinched the joint out. 'Come on: back to the grindstone.'

There was a long queue of small children and their parents between Craig and the grotto. A pasty-faced teenager dressed as an elf appeared in the door of Santa's little hideaway and ushered the first kid inside. Five minutes later the wee girl appeared out a side door, holding her mummy's hand and a small gift-wrapped parcel, looking back over her shoulder at the adulterous bastard in the red suit. And then the next child went in.

Craig joined the back of the queue. Watched another kid make the trip. Shuffled forwards. Checked his watch: fifteen kids, at five minutes a kid. . . At this rate it'd be over an hour before he got to sit on Santa's knee. The hell with that. He stepped out of line and lurched towards the grotto's exit.

'And what's your name little girl?'

'Hanna!' She squealed it out, so excited to be in Santa's house she couldn't stand still.

Stephen grinned at her, the weed mellowing everything into a rosy cosy glow. Greg could kiss his arse – this *was* groovy. 'Hello Hanna, and have you been a good girl this year?'

'Yeth!' Another lisp! Spectacular.

'And what would you like for—'

The exit door banged open and a man lurched in, bringing a smell of whisky with him.

Stephen was a total professional: kept up the big 'Ho,

Ho, Ho' voice and everything. 'I'm sorry, but Santa's busy with Hanna right now.'

The little girl giggled.

'You. . .' The man braced himself and squinted. 'You going to ask me if I've been naughty?'

OK – that wasn't good.

Stephen waved at Greg. 'Santa's little helper?'

Greg snapped off a military salute. 'Sah!'

'This man's lost, can you help him back to—'

'ASK ME IF I'VE BEEN NAUGHTY!'

Hanna stopped smiling and grabbed onto Stephen's leg.

Her mother narrowed wee squint eyes. 'Is this part of the show?'

'Er. . .' Stephen blinked. The first rule of Shopping Centre Santas was 'stay in character'. 'Well, I'd have to consult my list, I always check it twice, but—'

The man took two steps forward, snarling and slurring his words. '*I've* not been naughty, but *you* have, haven't you? WITH MY FUCKING WIFE!'

'What? Are you kidding? I'm married!'

'SO . . . AM . . . I!' Pounding his fist into his own chest between each word.

Oh shit – the guy was a nut. No way Stephen was getting the crap kicked out of him by a drunken bampot for minimum wage. Screw the code of the Santas. 'Look, mate, I don't know who you are, but I've never slept with your wife, OK? Come on, you're scaring the kid. . .'

And that was when the shotgun came out.

Craig brought the gun up until it was pointing right between the bastard's eyes. 'Liz told me all about it.' He flicked off the safety as the piped-in Christmas carols started in on 'Jingle Bells'. Tears made the room swim, even though he promised himself he wouldn't cry. 'Six months! SIX BLOODY MONTHS!'

The soon-to-be-dead Santa held his hands up, eyes wide. 'I never! I swear! Please!'

'You and her: after rehearsals for that fucking pipe band! Three times a week for six bloody months!' The gun was getting heavy, drifting down towards the floor.

'Mate, I never touched your wife: I'm not in a band. *I can't even play the spoons!*'

Craig screwed up his face, keeping the lying bastard in focus. 'I know it's you, she *told* me! You: Santa Fucking Claus!' He dragged the shotgun up again. 'Filling my wife's stockings!'

'Please!' Sweat trickled down Santa's face, into his beard. 'Not in front of the kids, eh?' He reached down and pulled the little girl. . . Hanna? Pulled Hanna round till she was standing in front of him. 'You don't want to ruin Christmas for her, do you?'

'No!' The woman leapt forwards, but Craig swung the gun round. She froze, trembling. 'Please, let me take my little girl! Please!'

Craig ignored her. 'Was she good?' he asked. 'My wife: was she good?'

'I never touched her, I swear!'

'She's only four!'

The idiot in the elf costume stuck up his hand. 'Maybe. . .' His voice cracked and he had to try again. 'Er. . . Maybe it's another Father Christmas? You know? They all look alike, right? With the beard and the hat and the belly?'

Craig squinted at him. 'Don't you *dare* patronize me!

She said she was screw . . . screwing the Santa down the shopping centre.' His sore hand throbbed – he shifted his grip on the shotgun.

'Which one?' The elf asked.

Craig opened his mouth, then frowned. Swore. There were *two* in the centre of town: the Guild Centre on Dean Street and this one. 'She didn't say.'

'See?' The guy with the beard slumped in his seat. 'I *told* you it wasn't me! I never touched your wife; it has to be the other Santa!' He covered his face with his hands. 'Oh thank Christ for that. . .'

'I. . .' Craig closed his eyes. The burrowing tick of a headache ate through the whisky numbness. How could he get it so *wrong*? He'd fucked it up, just like he fucked everything up. His one last, grand gesture was a total disaster.

The store would call the police, he'd be arrested, and the story would be all over the papers so everyone could see what a cretin he was. He'd go to prison and Liz would be free to screw the other Santa all day, every day. Laughing at stupid Craig the fuck-up. 'You *sure* you're not in the pipe band?'

'Positive.' The Santa forced a smile. 'Not in the band. It's not me!'

'Jingle Bells' finished and 'Deck the Halls with Boughs of Holly' started up instead. Fa la, la, la, la. . .

'I'm sorry. I didn't. . .' Should have known better. That's what he got for drinking all that whisky on an empty stomach. He wasn't thinking straight.

The shotgun was so heavy. Be good to put it down and just go to sleep.

'It's OK, easy mistake to make. I was just saying to—'

And that's when this deafening bang ripped through the grotto. Like a firework going off, or a car backfiring.

The left side of Santa's face disappeared in a spatter of red and grey.

Craig looked down at the gun in his hands.

Smoke drifted out from the end of the barrel. The woman started screaming, and the little girl cried, and the elf was sick in the corner.

Santa didn't even fall over: just sat there, held in place by the arms of the huge throne, leaking brains and blood into his beard. The wall behind him was pebble-dashed with bits of head. The whole place stank of sulphur, raw meat and fresh vomit.

He'd shot the wrong man. By accident.

He couldn't even fuck up properly.

Kinda funny when you thought about it.

Still, there was one thing he *could* do right. Craig sat on the floor, pulled out his bottle of Highland Park, and took a deep, long drink. Then placed the barrel under his chin and pulled the trigger.

Greg shivered in the corner, taking deep breaths, not looking at what was left of Liz's husband, Craig. Between him and Stephen, the place was like a horror movie.

He wiped a sticky chunk of red off the front of his stripy top. It left a long scarlet smear.

Thank Christ he'd exaggerated his job title when he told her about his new Christmas gig. After all: who wanted to shag an elf?

12: Drummers Drumming

There's a small pause – the kind you get before something really nasty happens – then all hell lets loose. From both ends.

'Oh Jesus. . .' I hold the horrible thing as far away from my suit as possible, but it's already too late: white milky vomit spatters all over my shoulder. Fresh urine sprays across my shirt and trousers. Soaking through to my skin. 'You little bast. . .'

I catch the look on Stephanie's face and turn it into a cough.

Forty-five-year-old men are not equipped to deal with small babies. It's not natural. And sticky. 'Oh Christ. . .' He's at it again, piddling like a broken teapot.

'Oh, give him here, for God's sake.' She reaches out and I hand over our first and only child – the way he's going there isn't likely to be a second one. Stephanie makes little cooing noises while I scramble out of my suit and into the last set of clean clothes I own: jeans and a tartan shirt. Like a bloody lumberjack, only grumpier.

111

Don't even have time to shower – going to be late as it is.

I throw the suit into the washing basket, kiss my wife on the cheek – it's Christmas Eve, I'm making the effort – and give my three-month-old son the best smile I can manage in the circumstances. Then leg it.

It's quarter past seven in the morning: Christmas Eve and the sky's burnt-toast black, dumping yet more snow on the city centre. Big fat flakes that melt to slush the moment they touch the gritty, shining tarmac.

My breath mists around my head as I hurry down the front steps to the waiting car.

PC Richardson's behind the wheel. He's a tall, stick-like man with the sort of face old ladies love. Not looking all that shiny this morning though, not with the bags under his swollen pink eyes, and stubble on his chin and cheeks.

He's got the radio on as I jump into the car.

'. . . concerned for the safety of Lord Peter Forsyth-Leven following his disappearance two days ago. In other news: a service of remembrance will be held at St. Jasper's Kirk today for drowned schoolgirl Danielle McArthur. We spoke to Danielle's family. . .'

Richardson cranks the volume down till the newscaster's voice disappears beneath the roar of the car's heater.

'Mornin', Guv.' His mouth droops. He sighs.

Normally I have to bash the cheerful bugger over the head with his own truncheon to make him settle down. I'm about to ask what's up when he wrinkles his nose and stares at my lumberjack ensemble.

They call me 'Stinky' behind my back.

They think I don't know, but I do. DI George 'Stinky' McClain. Bastards. It's not my fault: I've got a glandular condition. God knows how Stephanie puts up with it. I wash three times a day, use extra-strong deodorant, but the smell always leeches through in the end. Probably why I've got such a crap sense of smell. Self-defence.

At least this time I can blame the baby. But I don't: just snap on my seatbelt. 'You got that address?'

'Yup.' Another sigh: like he's deflating. 'Fourteen Denmuir Gardens, opposite the primary school.'

'Course it is. What a surprise.' I check the dashboard clock: eighteen minutes past seven. We're late.

There isn't much in the way of traffic: just a few vans making deliveries before the shops open; empty buses grumbling along dark, empty streets; one or two poor sods tramping their way to work through the falling snow.

And then we're out of the city centre, heading over the Calderwell Bridge. The Kings River sparkles like a vast slug beneath us, oozing its way out to the North Sea.

Kingsmeath isn't the nicest part of Oldcastle. It's a sprawl of council semis and tenement blocks thrown up in the sixties – and that's what they look like: concrete vomit. No wonder they're all crooks and junkies.

PC Richardson takes a left past Douglas on the Mound. The church's spire is covered in scaffolding, its walls covered in graffiti, its graveyard covered in snow. All the way out here and he's barely said a word. Maybe the real Richardson's been kidnapped by aliens and this is their half-arsed attempt at a replacement.

It takes us five minutes to find Denmuir Gardens: a dirt-streaked row of semi-detached houses with sagging roofs and satellite dishes. Halfway down, the street opens up: a mouldy playground sitting beside the single-storey concrete and rust-coloured lump that is KINGSMEATH PRIMARY SCHOOL.

Richardson parks the car and kills the engine while I pull out my handset and call control. 'Oscar Charlie, this is Charlie Hotel Six, we're in position.'

The speaker crackles. *'Roger that. You have a go as soon as all other units are in position. Good luck.'*

I stick it back in my pocket, then settle back in my seat, watching the house. The other unmarked CID cars and the dog handlers' van should be here in a minute.

Another big sigh from the passenger seat.

I smack Richardson on the arm. 'You've got a face like my mother-in-law's arse. Who died?'

He looks at me, then stares out at the snowflakes drifting down from the sky like flecks of gold in the streetlights' sulphurous glow. His eyes glisten, then a tear rolls down his cheek, his shoulders quiver, and the floodgates open. He sniffs. Wipes his eyes on the back of his sleeve. Apologizes for being so soft.

Jesus. That's not awkward, is it? For a moment, I just sit there. Then the man-management training kicks in and I reach over and squeeze his shoulder.

He looks at me, bottom lip quivering. 'I got a letter from my doctor.' He sniffs and wipes at his eyes again. 'Shite, I'm sorry. . . I . . . I gave blood last week.'

He takes a deep shuddering breath. 'I'm HIV positive.'

And I know it's stupid, and I know it's wrong, but I don't want to touch him anymore. Because I'm a shitty human being. Richardson's been on my team for years, he deserves better.

I squeeze his shoulder again. 'Are you OK?' It's a stupid question, but what am I supposed to do?

'I've never cheated on Sandra, I swear. It must've been . . . I don't know. . .'

In our job we come into contact with all sorts of sketchy bastards and their bodily fluids. All it takes is one drop of blood and you're screwed. Poor bastard.

'What's the FMO say?'

'I. . .' Richardson hangs his head. 'I only found out Wednesday . . . haven't told anyone. Not even Sandra. Oh God.' The tears were back. 'What am I going to tell her? What if I've *infected* her? What if I've given her AIDS?'

What the hell do you say to someone in that situation? 'Cheer up, could be worse'? I try for the shoulder squeeze again, but it doesn't help, he just cries all the harder. . .

Kilo Mike Two and Three finally arrive from the local Kingsmeath station.

Richardson takes one last shuddering breath and wipes his eyes. Trying to make out he's all right.

I fasten the Velcro on my bulletproof vest. 'I want you to stay here, OK? Keep an eye on the house while we go in.'

'No. I'm OK. You need the manpower.'

I shake my head. 'Not *that* much. You've had a shock. You. . .' Deep breath. 'What if something happens and you infect someone? Look, I'm sorry: I know it's shitty, but you've got to stay in the car.'

'No, I need to come with you, don't—'

'Believe me, I'd much rather have you with me than some of these KM Muppets, but you *have* to wait in the car. You know you do.'

'But—'

'We can talk about it when I get back, OK? Thain can

take the prisoners back to FHQ, and you and me will go grab a bacon buttie and talk, OK?'

'But—'

'No. You're staying put whether you like it or not.'

He goes back to staring at the falling snow. Sulking.

I can't really blame him.

A burgundy van pulls up in front of Kilo Mike Two – the dogs are here. That's my cue.

I climb out into the chilly morning air.

HIV. What a great end to the week. Still, after today I'm off till Tuesday. Three days of trudging around the three million relatives we never see at any other time of the year. Because 'everyone wants to see the baby'. Hell, I'm its dad and half the time even *I* don't want to see the little bugger.

DS Thain's waiting for me by the back of the dog van, dressed in firearms team black, machine pistol cradled against his chest. 'Morning, sir.' He eyes my lumberjack costume. 'Ready when you are.' He's one of these career policemen hot-footing it up the promotion ladder. But he's a nice guy, good cop too: efficient, not an arse-kisser like a lot of these fast-track wankers. Which makes it all the more unfair to take the piss out of his red hair.

But I do it anyway. 'Jesus, Thain, something horrible's happened to your head! Oh, wait, it's your hair.'

He smiles. 'Bugger off, sir.' Sounds a bit bunged up, as if he's got a cold.

I grin back at him. After PC Richardson and his cloud of impending doom, it's a bit of a relief.

DS Thain sniffs. 'What's the plan?'

'Surround the place. Half the troops round the back, everyone else round the front. Two from each team go

116

in, the rest wait outside in case Black makes a run for it.' I look up at the house, then back at the Canine Unit where the black nose of a police Alsatian is making snotty whorls on the glass. 'And we're taking one of the dogs in with us too. Just in case.'

'Sir.' He marches off to get everyone in place, red hair glowing in the gloom.

I give Stephanie a ring and ask if she wants anything from the shops while I'm out. Still making the effort.

Stephanie doesn't want anything. But she *almost* sounds happy I called. We chat for a bit about who's getting what for Christmas. No fights. No sniping. Just two grownups having a conversation. Who knows: maybe if we can make it through to the New Year there's hope for us after all. We could—

DS Thain is back, giving me the thumbs up.

I nod, then shift the phone to my other ear. 'Sorry, I gotta go. See you at four.'

'*Love you.*'

'Love you too.' Because I still do.

And then it's time to get going.

Life is beginning to stir in Denmuir Gardens: lights sparkling on in lounge windows, bedrooms and kitchens. But not number fourteen. Dillon Black is obviously having a bit of a lie-in.

He's about to get rudely awakened.

'Right: everyone make sure your partner's got their vest on – there's no record of Black owning a gun, but we're not taking any chances. I expect Black to resist, but he's not an idiot. He pulls a gun and we'll blow his arse off. He puts up a fight and the dogs will tear him a new one. His only choice is to come quietly.'

The firearms team check their Heckler and Koch MP5 machine pistols and Glock 9mms.

'I want this nice and clean, people. No heroics, no shooting things for the fun of it. In and out: no one hurt. Understand?'

They 'Yes sir!' me, then everyone trots off into place, coughing and sneezing as they go. You can always tell when it's Christmas in Oldcastle because every bugger on day shift is dying from colds and flu.

Thain nods towards the car Richardson's sitting in. 'Not letting him out to play?'

I shrug. 'He's not feeling well.'

'Oh aye?' Thain blows his nose, just to make sure I know that *he's* not feeling too hot either. Tough. He racks a round into the chamber of his machine pistol.

I give the signal.

The battering ram rips the front door right off its hinges. BOOM. It falls back into the hallway in a flurry of splintered wood. The place is in darkness, and it's cold too – like the central heating hasn't come on yet. Which makes sense: the kind of business Dillon Black runs doesn't keep nine-to-five hours. It happens after dark in deserted car parks and warehouses.

I lead the way, stepping into the hall as another BOOM sounds from round the back: the second team coming in. Thain and I charge up the stairs in the darkness, following the glow from the torches strapped to our MP5s.

'POLICE, COME OUT WITH YOUR HANDS UP!'

First door's a bathroom, second's a box room full of DVD players and cases of whisky, third's a bedroom – empty – and so is number four. No sign of anyone.

Thain sweeps his torch beam back and forth. 'Where the hell is he?'

'Check the attic, we might get lucky.' But we won't: Dillon Black's not here.

There's nothing but junk in the attic, so we check all the bedroom cupboards then head back downstairs. There's a small clump of constables at the foot of the stairs, hands in their pockets, helmets tucked under their arms, arguing about whether or not Oldcastle Warriors are the worst football team in Scotland. Passing round a packet of cigarettes. They've come up empty-handed as well.

Thain peers into the lounge. 'Someone must've tipped him off.'

Wouldn't be the first time.

I shrug and wander through. It's a big enough room: widescreen TV, fancy stereo, one of the DVD recorders from the stash upstairs . . . but something's wrong. The chairs are all turned to face a blank wall with a nail in it. Like they've been looking at something that doesn't hang there anymore.

Thain turns in place, sniffing the air. 'Can you smell something funny?'

Great. Bad enough the bastards do it behind my back, I never thought Thain would be the kind of arsehole to play it up in front of the troops.

I poke him in the chest. 'It's not my bloody fault, OK? The baby was sick on me this morning, he peed all down my suit. I didn't have time to shower! You bunch of—'

My phone starts ringing. I drag it out. 'WHAT?'

There's a 'scccchrickt' from the hall: the sound of a sly fag being lit.

A pause from the other end of the line, then, '*Sir, it's Richardson. You have to get out of there.*'

Thain's frowning, 'No, it's not you, it's more . . . can you smell gas?'

'*Sir, I mean it, you—*'

'Oh, for God's sake, *Richardson*: I'm not telling you again. Stay in the bloody car!'

'Sccccchrickt'

'*Sir! You have to—*'

I freeze. 'Wait, what? Gas?' I can't smell anything, but then I never could.

'Sccccchrickt'

'*Sir?*'

'Sccccchrickt'

The world slows down. Every single detail stands out like a knife blade: the patch of stubble on Thain's chin; the laughter coming from the hall; the DVD case for *The Muppet Christmas Carol* lying on the carpet; the sound of my heart beating in my ears like a drum. Thump, thump, thump.

I turn, haul in a deep breath. 'NO!' And then everything

PC Richardson made it as far as the garden gate before the house blew. A sudden rush of heat and noise, blasting through the lounge window, spraying him with broken of glass, knocking him flat on his back. And then the flames, roaring over his head as he lay in the middle of the snow-covered pavement.

He groaned. Rolled over onto his side, then up onto his knees. It wasn't meant to happen like this!

Ewan Richardson staggered to his feet and stared at

what was left of Dillon Black's house. The whole downstairs was gone and a good chunk of upstairs too. Bricks and bits of wood littered the front garden. A police-issue helmet lay halfway down the garden path. Someone's arm poked out through the front door.

Richardson lurched forwards, peering into what was left of the lounge. It was covered in blood and bits of dark-red meat.

He put one hand against the wall and threw up in the snow.

It wasn't meant to be like this: *he* was supposed to go in first. Flick on the lights. . .

No one else was meant to get hurt. Just him. Blown to pieces instead of lingering on, getting sicker and sicker. Watching his body slowly kill itself. IT WAS MEANT TO BE HIM!

He sank down against the wall.

It should've been him.

A cheerful blast of music came from his pocket. He dragged out his mobile phone: Sandra. Richardson switched it off without taking the call, covered his face with his hands and sobbed.

He should be dead now – quick and painless – and Sandra would get his death in service benefits, and his pension. A big chunk of money to look after her and little Emma. To say sorry. For everything.

Now all she'd get was the £3,000 Dillon Black had paid him for the warning about this morning's raid.

Life was so unfair.